Mia's recipe for disaster

SIMON SPOTLIGHT

An imprint of Simon & Schuster Children's Publishing Division
1230 Avenue of the Americas, New York, New York 10020
First Simon Spotlight paperback edition October 2014
Copyright © 2014 by Simon & Schuster, Inc. All rights reserved,
including the right of reproduction in whole or in part in any form.
SIMON SPOTLIGHT and colophon are registered
trademarks of Simon & Schuster, Inc.
Text by Tracey West
Chapter header illustrations by Maryam Choudhury
Designed by Laura Roode
For information about special discounts for bulk purchases, please contact
Simon & Schuster Special Sales
at 1-866-506-1949 or business@simonandschuster.com.
Manufactured in the United States of America 0914 OFF
2 4 6 8 10 9 7 5 3 1
ISBN 978-1-4814-1864-5 (pbk)
ISBN 978-1-4814-1865-2 (hc)
ISBN 978-1-4814-1866-9 (eBook)
Library of Congress Catalog Card Number 2014945245

CUPCAKE DIARIES

Mia's recipe for disaster

by coco simon

Simon Spotlight
New York London Toronto Sydney New Delhi

CHAPTER 1

My Big Break!

$\mathcal{A}$ ll right, people! Hit the lockers!" called out Ms. Chen, our gym teacher.

I jogged off the basketball court along with my friends Katie, Emma, and Alexis. We all have gym together, which is great. We all have pretty complicated feelings about gym, though.

Emma is blonde, sweet, a little shy, and gorgeous—and, surprisingly, a competitive beast when she plays sports. I think it comes from having three brothers. She especially gets mad when the girls and boys play together and the boys don't pass the ball to the girls.

"What do they think? That we're not as good as them?" she'd say.

Alexis is competitive, too, but mostly about

academic things. She likes gym—mainly because she's really good at it—but she just loves to criticize it. "You need a healthy body to maintain a healthy mind," she'd always say. "But gym class is just not an efficient way to get exercise. Half the time we're standing around, waiting to play."

Then there's my best friend, Katie. She used to hate gym more than I hate polyester, mostly because she used to get teased because she wasn't good at sports. But she's a lot more confident now.

"Can you believe I made a basket today?" she was saying as we walked toward the locker room. She jumped up, pretending to make an imaginary layup. "An actual basket. In gym!"

"You did great, Katie," Emma said.

"I almost wish gym wasn't over yet," Katie said, and I gave her a look.

"Did you actually just say that?" I asked.

"Well, I said 'almost,'" Katie replied.

"Well, I am definitely glad it's over," I said. "That means I can get out of this uniform."

I am at war with my Park Street Middle School gym uniform. For one thing, it's half polyester, which is just itchy and gross. Polyester makes me sweat more, which is the exact opposite of what I need in a gym uniform. As Alexis would say, it's not logical.

Then there are the shorts, which balloon out on the sides like old-fashioned bloomers. And it's a totally boring blue color, not a deep navy or a pretty powder blue, but just this really dull blue, a dirty grayish blue, like the color of the sky on a drizzly day. Blah.

"Mia, you look great in the uniform," Katie said. "You look great in everything."

"Thanks, but nobody looks good in this," I said. I pulled at the fabric of the shorts. "I took these to my last class at Parsons, and Millicent, a design student, showed me how to alter the seam, so they don't look so baggy. But they're still hideous!"

Parsons is a pretty famous design school in New York City. My mom signed me up for a class there, which is totally awesome.

By now we had reached the locker room and quickly got changed for next period: lunch. We only get about three minutes to change, which is ridiculous. I never have time to redo my hair, which is always all over the place after gym.

"How is that class going, anyway?" Alexis asked.

"Really good," I said. "I'm learning so much about sewing. Which I'm going to need to do if I'm serious about becoming a fashion designer."

"Oh, you're definitely serious about it, all right,"

Katie said with a grin. "It's all you talk about."

"Not all," I said, but then I remembered something. "Oh! I have something to show you guys at lunch. I found out about it yesterday, and I'm so excited!"

"Yesterday? Why didn't you tell me on the bus this morning?" Katie asked.

"I wanted to save it and tell everybody at lunch," I told her. "This could totally be my big break."

Katie raised her eyebrows. "Tell us now!"

"Not in this smelly locker room," I said, and then the bell rang. "Come on, let's go to lunch!"

The four of us pushed our way through a sea of middle schoolers as we headed to the cafeteria. Once we got there, Katie and I went to our usual table, and Alexis and Emma got on the food line.

"Come on, just tell me now," Katie said as she unwrapped her PB&J sandwich.

I shook my head. "You are so impatient!" I told her, laughing.

Katie put down her sandwich and closed her eyes. "Okay. I'll just meditate until you're ready then."

That's when Alexis and Emma walked up, carrying trays of salad.

"What's with Katie?" Emma asked.

4

"I'm meditating," Katie said.

"Not if you're talking," I pointed out.

"Meditation can be very beneficial," Alexis said. "In Business Club we learned that many successful executives practice it. It keeps them focused."

Katie opened her eyes. "Okay, I'm focused. Now tell us, Mia!"

I opened my backpack and took out a magazine, *Teen Runway*. I flipped through the pages and stopped at a photo of a model gliding down a runway in a gorgeous chiffon evening gown. The headline above her read, "Design Your Fantasy Dress—Enter Our Contest!"

"*Teen Runway* is having a contest," I told my friends. "It's open to anyone between the ages of twelve and sixteen. You have to create a dress that you would wear to a fashion event with all the top designers. The grand prize is a thousand bucks, but that's not even the best part. The winner gets their dress photographed on a professional model for the magazine, plus a meeting with famous designers."

I put the magazine down on the table, so everyone could see. "I can totally do this," I said. "Especially now that I'm taking that sewing class. You have to sew your dress yourself and send in a picture of it for the contest."

"You can totally *win* this," Katie said, excited.

"Totally," Emma agreed, nodding.

"It's the perfect contest for you," Alexis said. "Although I wonder how many people will be competing. Do you know how many subscribers the magazine has? Maybe we could estimate."

"I think maybe it's better if you don't think about the other competitors," Emma suggested. "Just bring your amazing vision to life."

I nodded. "Exactly! On every fashion competition show I've watched, people get in trouble when they worry about what other people are doing."

"So, can you do the sewing at your class in the city?" Katie asked.

"That's my plan," I said. "This week, I'm here with Mom. I can spend the time sketching and figuring out what material I need. Then next weekend I'm at Dad's, so I can work on the pattern there."

My parents are divorced, so every other weekend I take the train to New York City, where I used to live, and hang out with my dad. The rest of the time I live here in Maple Grove with my mom; my stepdad, Eddie; and Dan, my stepbrother. It used to be much more confusing, but we all figured it out, and now it just seems normal.

Katie scrunched up her face. "I almost forgot.

Will you be around the weekend of George's Halloween party?"

"Yes. And even if I wasn't, I would ask Dad if I could go. I definitely don't want to miss that."

Suddenly, George Martinez appeared at our lunch table.

"So are you guys all going to dress up like cupcakes for my party?" he asked.

Katie almost jumped out of her chair. "George! We were just talking about you. That is so weird."

George waggled his eyebrows. "Really! Were you talking about how cute I am?"

Katie blushed, because she *does* think George is cute. Which is okay because he thinks Katie is cute too. You can totally tell.

"No," she said. "We were talking about your party."

"And we are *not* going as cupcakes," I said. "That would be ridiculous." But I understood why George suggested it. My friends and I formed a cupcake club when we started middle school. We bake cupcakes for parties and other events. Everyone in school pretty much knows us as "the Cupcakers."

"Actually, it's a pretty cool idea," Katie said. "Although it might be kind of hard to go to the bathroom in a giant cupcake costume."

George laughed. "Yeah, right. But you're all coming, right?"

"Yes!" we all answered at once.

"Good," George said, and he headed back to his lunch table.

"*Everybody* is going to that party," Alexis said, leaning in toward us.

"I know," Emma said, her blue eyes shining. "The last time I went to a boy-girl party at somebody's house, it was, like, first grade or something."

Katie nudged me. "Is Chris going?"

Now it was my turn to blush. "I'm not sure," I said. "He hasn't texted me in a while."

Chris Howard is this boy in my grade who I'm pretty sure I like. He's tall and cute, and he has braces like I do, only mine are the clear kind, and he has the shiny metal kind. But they don't make him any less cute.

Emma was frowning. "I haven't thought about a costume yet. If we don't go as cupcakes, what will we go as?"

"If I didn't have this contest, I would design fabulous costumes for all of us," I said. "Sorry."

"No, the contest is way more important," Katie said, and Emma and Alexis nodded in agreement.

8

Then Alexis opened up her planner. "So, Cupcake Club meeting at your house, Mia? Saturday?"

I nodded. "Mom and Eddie said fine. We could get pizza, or Eddie said he'd make spaghetti for us."

"Eddie's spaghetti!" Katie sang out. "It's delicious, and besides, it rhymes."

Alexis looked at the clock. "Ten minutes until the bell rings, and we haven't eaten a bite." She picked up her fork and dug into her salad.

I picked up my turkey wrap in one hand and stared at the magazine page in my other hand.

If I win this contest, it could change everything, I thought. *I could go from middle schooler to fashion designer overnight!*

CHAPTER 2

Spooky Sketches

When I actually sat down to start sketching that night, creating my fantasy dress was way harder than I thought. What did it actually mean to make a "fantasy dress"? Should it be sophisticated, like something you'd wear to an art gallery opening, or runway-ready glamorous?

And even though I had said that I didn't want to worry about what other people might do, I *was* kind of worried. It was so hard to keep up with all the changing trends. Not that I wanted to follow them, but I knew I had to be ahead of them. My mom is a stylist, which means she helps pick out outfits and whole wardrobes for people. She helps magazines figure out which clothes to show, or she will help actresses with their wardrobes for a TV show or movie. She even styles "regular" people too. It's pretty cool. Anyway, Mom was always talking about "being on trend," so I know it's important.

I opened up my laptop and started searching for the fall runway shows. My head was pretty much in Paris when Mom stepped in through the open doorway.

"Mia, did you finish your homework?" she asked.

"I just have one worksheet to do," I said, quickly closing the window on my screen so Mom wouldn't see the model in the slinky sequined gown. But she already had me figured out.

"Honey, I know you're excited about the contest, but school first, okay?"

I sighed. "Yes." I shut the laptop. But inside I was thinking, *If I win that contest, school won't matter!* Which, okay, to be honest, deep down I knew wasn't true, but it was still fun to dream.

I quickly finished my homework and then went back online. There were so many trends: hot pants with blazers, retro-looking dresses, lots of leather and fake fur. How was I supposed to come up with the *next* big thing?

As I flopped down onto my bed, Mom came back in.

"Bedtime, Mia. Laptop off, please."

"I know," I said, but I didn't move. I was too depressed. Mom sat down next to me.

"What's wrong?" she asked.

"I don't know how designers do it," I said. "How do you create something that nobody's ever done before and that everybody wants?"

Mom thought for a moment. She knows a lot of designers. "As a stylist, I listen to what my clients want and then try to find a designer who shares that same kind of style. Most designers have a specific style. The most successful ones have a style that appeals to a lot of people and that is wearable for a lot of people. I love leopard-print jumpsuits, but that is not something everyone can pull off."

I shuddered, imagining some of my friends' moms wearing leopard-print jumpsuits. "Yeah, not a good look for normal everyday wear."

"Talk to your friends," Mom suggested. "Find out what they would want in a fantasy dress. It may spark some ideas."

"That's a great idea!" I said, jumping up. I rooted under my bed and pulled out some fashion magazines from the stack that has piled up under there. Then I stuffed them into my backpack. "I can ask them at our Cupcake meeting on Saturday. Oh by the way, they want Eddie to make his spaghetti."

Mom smiled. "He'll be thrilled."

Mom said good night, and I got ready for bed. That night I dreamed I was walking down a runway, wearing my gym uniform, leopard-print boots, and a fake-fur vest.

I can't believe I didn't wake up screaming!

Convincing my friends to help me out was easy. But it was almost as if Katie *wanted* to give me a hard time. When I handed her some magazines to look through at lunch the next day, she looked at me like I was handing her a dirty sock.

"So you want us to do what?" she asked.

I handed her a purple marker. "Just look through it and circle the stuff you like. Stuff you might wear. You don't have to do it now—just bring it Saturday."

"Ooh, this is going to be fun!" Emma said.

"Are you sure you want *me* to do this?" Katie asked. Her idea of dressing up is to wear a clean pair of jeans with her T-shirt and sneakers. But once in a while she lets me pick out clothes for her, and she looks totally adorable.

"Yes, *you*," I insisted.

My friends didn't disappoint me. Saturday at five o'clock, the house smelled like tomato sauce and garlic, and when the doorbell rang, my dogs, Tiki and Milkshake, started yapping like crazy. When I opened the door, Katie, Emma, and Alexis were standing there, carrying the magazines I had given them.

They came inside, and Katie bent down to pet the dogs. They adore her.

"Emma, how was your modeling thing?" I asked. She gets professional modeling gigs sometimes.

"Another catalog," Emma said. "Winter coats. And it felt like ninety degrees in the studio. Gross!"

"Well, I got pretty sweaty during the race this morning," Katie said.

"Did your mom and Mr. Green run too?" I asked. Katie's mom is dating a math teacher, Mr. Green, in our school. It's really nice, but weird for Katie. Katie and her mom run, and Mr. Green does too, so now they all run together sometimes.

"Yes, and Emily, too," Katie said—Emily is Mr. Green's daughter—and grinned. "But I beat them all."

"So how do you want to do this?" Alexis asked. "Fashion first or cupcakes first?"

"Let's do fashion, then spaghetti, and then talk about cupcakes for dessert," Katie suggested. "It's, you know, fitting."

"Okay, let's go to my room," I said.

I had cleaned up my room (well, I shoved a few things under the bed), but I keep it pretty clean because I have loved it ever since Eddie helped me redo it. The walls are turquoise, and Eddie and I painted over the old furniture a glossy white, with black trim. Mom helped me with the colors but mostly it was my design.

I tossed some turquoise and fuchsia throw pillows from my bed to the floor.

"Okay, let's see what you've got," I told my friends.

"Me first!" Emma said, handing me a magazine. "I found tons of beautiful dresses in here."

I flipped through the pages. The dresses she had circled with the pink marker I gave her were—what else?—pink and fluffy, or they had floral prints.

"These are so *you*," I told her. "So, do you think 'romantic' would be a good way to describe your style? Or 'sweet and flirty'?"

Emma nodded. "Definitely," she said, looking down at the white peasant top and pink skirt she was wearing.

"Well, I didn't circle anything with flowers," Alexis said. She handed me back the stack of magazines I had given her, with the pages neatly flagged.

"The ones I liked best looked nice, but they were practical, too."

Katie frowned. "You mean like uniforms?"

"No, I mean—well, turn to page thirty-seven of that one," Alexis said, pointing, and I quickly obeyed. "See that black dress? You can wear it to work during the day, and then you can dress it up and wear it to a party at night. It says it right here: 'One dress, two different looks, pretty and practical!'"

I nodded. "My mom's clients love stuff like that."

Then I looked at Katie. "Sooooo . . ."

Katie sighed and handed me the magazines. "Well, I didn't find my fantasy dress. I found some stuff I wouldn't mind wearing, though."

Looking through the pages, I saw that Katie circled a lot of pictures of models wearing jeans and shirts, or shorts and shirts. No surprise there.

"Well, what would your fantasy dress look like?" I asked.

"I was thinking about that," Katie said. "I guess if I had a really special thing to go to, I would want something completely different and amazing. Like a dress with a rainbow swirl all around it, or maybe a silver space-looking dress with a hat that had spirals coming out of it."

Alexis laughed. "I could so see you in that!"

"I tried to draw it, but it came out terrible," Katie said.

But I was already sketching. After a minute I held out my sketch pad to Katie.

"Like this?" I asked.

Katie looked at my drawing, which showed a sleeveless dress that was short in the front and long in the back. The hat on the figure I had drawn was a small cap topped with a twisting spiral, kind of like what DNA looks like.

Katie's brown eyes lit up. "That is awesome!"

"I think it might be too . . . creative for this contest," I said. "But it's really fun. I will totally design that for you someday."

"You'd better!" Katie said.

Then we heard Eddie's voice call up the stairs. "Who wants some of Eddie's spaghetti?"

"Meeeee!" Katie yelled back, and she raced out of the room ahead of all of us.

Downstairs, we all sat at the dining room table with my mom and Eddie. The table was topped with big bowls of food: spaghetti, meatballs, salad, and a basket of garlic bread.

"Where's Dan?" Emma asked.

"Basketball practice," Eddie replied. "But that just means more spaghetti for us!"

"Well, we should save some for poor Dan when he comes home starving," Mom interjected with a laugh, and started passing around the bowls, and we piled food onto our plates.

"Thanks for making spaghetti for us," Katie said, twirling the pasta around her fork. "One of these days you need to tell me the recipe for your sauce."

"Well, it's a secret recipe, but for you I might make an exception," Eddie told her with a wink.

"I can repay you in cupcakes," Katie promised.

"Are you girls baking tonight?" Mom asked.

I shook my head. "No. Just talking business."

"Jake's best friend, Angelo Ricco, is having a Halloween party," Emma explained. "Last week his mom asked me if we could bake Halloween cupcakes for it."

"This is going to be so much fun!" Katie said. "Mia, I bet you can come up with amazing Halloween designs."

Normally, I would have been excited too, but honestly, cupcakes were the last things on my mind. All I really wanted to do was figure out a design for my contest dress. But I didn't want to let down my Cupcake Club friends.

"I haven't thought of anything yet, but I can start sketching after dinner," I said.

"And I've been researching Halloween cupcake designs online," Alexis reported. "I downloaded my favorites."

"You girls impress me," Eddie said. "You've got a great little business going here."

"And it's fueled by Eddie's spaghetti!" Katie added, just before she slurped a long strand of pasta into her mouth.

Eddie laughed. Since he was used to living with just Dan for a while, I don't think he knew what to do with a house full of girls at first, but now he totally loves it when my friends come over. It doesn't hurt that we all love his cooking.

After we ate, we cleaned up the table and then got ready for our meeting. I got my sketchbook and some colored pencils, Alexis had a laptop open, and Katie had a purple binder with cupcake stickers all over it. It was Alexis's idea. Katie used to just shove her favorite cupcake recipes into a pocket into her backpack. Now they're neatly organized (well, as neatly as Katie can organize anything).

"So, Mrs. Ricco wants four dozen cupcakes," Emma began. "She's inviting, like, the whole first grade."

"Because it's little kids, we might want to do

simple flavors," Alexis suggested. "Vanilla and chocolate."

"Maybe we could do a dozen pumpkin ones?" Katie asked. "It's Halloween, and everybody loves pumpkin."

"Yes! Do pumpkin!" Eddie called from the kitchen, and we all laughed.

"Eddie, no input from nonmembers!" I yelled back, but I didn't really mind. Eddie's sweet, and if I have to have a stepdad, I'm glad it's him.

"Vanilla, chocolate, and pumpkin," Alexis said, making a note. "What about decorations?"

"I think we could do a whole bunch of different ones," Emma suggested. "Jake loves anything with a lot of colors, so I think they'd like something fun."

Alexis turned the laptop around and showed us a screen with a grid of the photos of Halloween cupcakes she had found. The designs were really cool. Some cupcakes had orange icing and candy faces that made them look like jack-o'-lanterns; others had white icing with lacy black spiderweb designs on top. I even saw some vampire faces drawn on with icing, with little candy fangs.

"I want to do them all!" Katie said.

Seeing all the pictures got me really inspired. I started sketching like crazy.

"We could do a cemetery cupcake," I said. "Chocolate icing, with cookie tombstones on top. We could write 'RIP' on each one."

"Cool!" Katie said. "But is that too scary for little kids?"

"Well, we could do some fun monsters," I continued, still sketching. "With funky-colored icing, like purple and lime green. We could use candy to make the faces."

And the ideas kept coming. "Oh, what if we used those thin licorice whips to make spider legs?" I said. "See? The round cupcake is the body of the spider. We could stick four legs on each side. Then we could get those little candy eyes they sell and put them where the eyes would go. Or draw them on with icing."

Katie hugged me. "That is why you are going to win that contest," she said. "There is nobody out there as creative as you."

I could feel myself blush. "You're my best friend. You have to say that. But . . . it doesn't mean I don't love hearing it."

"Well, I agree," Alexis said. "If you can tap into your creativity, your dress is sure to be a winner."

Emma nodded. "You're going to do great, Mia."

I know it might sound a little conceited, but

21

I agreed with them. I knew I could make a great dress—a winning dress. It's in my blood, thanks to Mom. It's what I was born to do.

I couldn't wait to get started!

CHAPTER 3

Trouble with Katie ☺

$\mathcal{I}$ ended up filling an entire sketchbook with ideas for my fantasy dress. I thought about what my friends liked, and I sketched a superflouncy, pink, flowery dress that Emma would like, and a dress with removable sleeves for Alexis. I still had cupcakes on my mind, and I made a dress with lace spiderwebs all over the front, but that definitely looked like a costume. (Although I know Katie would have loved it.)

But the inspiration for my final dress didn't hit me until I was in the shower one night. I'm not sure why it happened—maybe it was the soothing sound of the water or the warm steam, but suddenly all the confusing thoughts cleared out of my head and I knew exactly what I needed to do.

I was so excited to sketch it out that I didn't even dry my hair! I quickly combed it and then sat down at my desk and got to work. When I was done, I knew it was the right one. I could feel it in my bones.

I put the sketch neatly in a folder and tucked it into my backpack. The next day at school, my hair was frizzy, but I didn't care. I couldn't wait to show the sketch to my friends.

I didn't talk about the sketch at all until lunch. After everyone ate, I made my announcement.

"I have something to show you," I said. "I finished my sketch for my fantasy dress. Ta-daaaa!"

I took out the sketch from the folder and held it up. I was so proud! The idea I had come up with was sort of a little bit Emma and a little bit Alexis. The main piece was a long, strapless gray evening gown. The design was pretty simple, but I had added a slit on the right side, which would reveal that the dress was lined in pink satin. Then I had designed a short cape that could go with the dress. It was gray on one side and pink on the other.

"It's so pretty!" Emma squealed.

Alexis leaned closer. "So the cape is reversible? I like that. It's like getting two capes in one."

"Exactly," I said. "And, Emma, when you walk in it, you'll be able to see the pink lining through the slit."

"It's gorgeous," Emma said. "Sophisticated and sweet at the same time. And the pink is subtle, so you have to really look at the dress or watch someone walk in it to see it. Like a little secret."

"Would you want people to watch you walk the whole night?" Katie joked, but nobody was really paying attention to her. Emma and Alexis were oohing and aahing over the dress, and I was just taking it all in. I felt really great about what I had designed.

Then Katie piped up again. "It's nice," she said hesitantly. "But I'm not sure if it's contest worthy, you know? I mean, don't get me wrong, it's really pretty, but it's . . . plain. And when I watch that fashion contest show with you on TV, those dresses that win are always complicated and have interesting features. The simple stuff doesn't get much attention. I'm just saying."

I couldn't help feeling annoyed. Emma and Alexis saw how special the dress was—why couldn't Katie, my best friend?

"It's deceptively simple," I explained. "The pink lining is going to be satin, which is an extremely difficult fabric to work with. It's very slippery and bunches up easily, so it takes real talent to line a dress with it smoothly."

Katie nodded. "I get it. I'm just saying that to win you might need something that looks more . . . spectacular. I don't know. Some sequins, maybe? A big pink bow or shiny ribbons somewhere?"

I sighed. I love Katie, but she doesn't know anything about fashion. She *didn't* get it—that was the whole problem. And I didn't feel like I had to explain myself to her. I mean, I've devoted my whole life to fashion.

"It doesn't *need* any bows or sequins," I said. Then because I was still feeling annoyed, I added, "And it's kind of funny that you, of all people, have such a strong opinion on this. I mean, *your* biggest fashion decision is usually which T-shirt is clean enough to throw on with your faded jeans."

I gave a little laugh when I said it, but from the expression on Katie's face, I could tell she didn't think it was funny. I quickly changed the subject and turned to Emma.

"Emma, the contest rules say I have to send a photo of someone wearing my creation," I told her. "Will you model my dress for me?"

Then I looked at Alexis. She recently grew, like,

three inches overnight (or that's what it seemed like, anyway), and now she has this perfect body for modeling clothes.

"Or you could do it, too, Alexis! A gray gown would look gorgeous with your red hair!"

"Wow, that's flattering," Alexis said. "But Emma is the real model of the group. She should definitely do it."

Emma smiled shyly. "I would love to model for you."

Fortunately, I always carry a measuring tape with me, so I jumped up.

"Stand up, Emma!" I commanded. "I need to take your measurements so I know what size to make the dress."

Emma giggled. "Mia, we're in the middle of the cafeteria! Did you forget?"

"Nobody will notice," I said.

"Everybody will notice," countered Alexis.

"Anyway, I just had my measurements taken for my last modeling job. I'll write them down for you, okay?" Emma asked.

I sat down and slid my sketchbook over to Emma. "Thanks."

Emma picked up the book and then looked over at Katie. She was extremely focused on a chocolate pudding cup, jabbing a plastic spoon into it over and over again.

"Katie, what's wrong?" Emma asked.

Katie put down her spoon and looked right at me. "So I guess I'm not pretty enough to model your dress? Well, don't worry. I wouldn't want to wear your boring gray dress, anyway."

At first, I just got mad that Katie called my dress boring. Then I realized I had asked Emma and Alexis to model, and not Katie. No wonder her feelings got hurt.

I tried to apologize—honestly, I did—but I guess I made it worse.

"Katie, I didn't mean it like that!" I protested. "It's just . . . you're not really into fashion, and of course you're pretty enough, but clothes look better on people who are tall; that's just a fact. And you also need to be graceful, and you know how you are in gym class and everything. You know how George calls you Silly Arms? And you can't have silly arms on the runway. . . ."

Alexis and Emma were waving their arms wildly behind Katie—not because they were goofing on her Silly Arms nickname, but because they wanted me to stop talking. I didn't realize it, though. The whole time I thought I was making it better, I was just making it worse and worse. Katie's face was as red as an apple.

"Mia, stop," Alexis said quietly. "Just . . . *stop.*"

But it was too late. Katie stood up, and I saw tears streaming down her face.

She turned and left the cafeteria without another word.

CHAPTER 4

I Live for Fashion!

$\mathcal{I}$ felt guilty and angry at the same time.

"She didn't have to get so upset!" I told Emma and Alexis, who were looking at me accusingly.

"It was just a misunderstanding," Emma said in that sweet way of hers. "But you should find her and apologize."

That just made me angrier. "Me? She's the one who called my dress boring! I never said she wasn't pretty enough to model my dress. Where did she get that from?"

"Well, it was kind of weird you asked us and you didn't ask her," Alexis pointed out.

"Are you serious? Katie hates fashion! Why would she even want to model?" I asked.

Alexis frowned thoughtfully. "You have a point."

"But you should still try to make up with her," Emma added. "She might not have wanted to do it, but that doesn't mean she didn't want to get asked, anyway. And she looked so upset when she left."

I sighed. "I guess."

But then the bell rang, and I had to get to my next class. I figured I could talk to Katie before fifth period, when we both have social studies with Mrs. Kratzer.

When I got to class, Katie wouldn't even look up at me. That just made me mad again. If she wouldn't look at me, why would I talk to her? The same thing happened during sixth period science with Ms. Chandar.

The fact that Katie didn't even *look* at me really hurt. But she's my best friend here in Maple Grove, so I figured we could sort it out on the bus. Only when I went out to catch the bus, I saw Katie get into a small red car. I'd seen it before. Sometimes she gets picked up by Joanne, a woman who works at the dentist office run by Katie's mom, Mrs. Brown.

I couldn't believe it. Was this something already planned, or had Katie arranged the ride so she could avoid me? I almost felt like crying myself.

But I couldn't let it get to me. I had a busy weekend ahead of me. Once I got home, I quickly packed for my weekend at Dad's, and then Mom drove me to the train station.

It only takes about an hour to get from Maple Grove to Manhattan on the train. It goes fast because I put in my earbuds and sketch, and usually, nobody bothers me. Plus, my mom and dad tell me not to talk to anyone, and they each text me about once a minute to make sure I'm okay. Once in a while I'll get an old lady who will act like she doesn't notice my earbuds and will want to strike up a conversation, but today I got lucky, and nobody sat in the seat next to me for the whole ride.

That gave me time to plan out a list of what I needed to do before I got back on the train on Sunday. Alexis would have been proud.

Saturday
9:00: go to fabric shop with Ava
11:00: design class at Parsons
1:00: Dad picks us up and takes us to lunch

Actually, when I wrote it down, it didn't look like much. But those first two things were really important. I had to find just the right fabrics for my dress, and then I had to try to finish the pattern during class, because I knew I wouldn't get there again for two weeks!

"Mia, I'm so excited!" Ava said as she ran down the front steps of her building the next morning.

"Me too!" I cried, hugging her. "You have to help me find the perfect material for my dress."

Behind me, Dad yawned and took a sip of his coffee. "I can't believe the fabric store is open so early."

"It's never too early for fashion!" I said, and then Ava and I burst into giggles.

Ava is my other best friend—sort of the Manhattan Katie, except Ava and Katie aren't much alike. They're both nice and funny and sweet, but Ava loves sports, and she's into clothes as much as I am. That's why she agreed to take the class at Parsons with me.

Dad took us to the subway, and twenty minutes later we had traveled from downtown Manhattan to midtown west, where the Garment District is located. The streets there are filled with shops where you can buy fabric and zippers and trim and anything else you need to design clothes. Mom told us that we should go to a place called L&M Fabrics.

33

We walked up from the subway station into the bright morning sunlight.

"It should be just up here," Dad said, looking at the street numbers on the shops. Then he stopped. "Ah, here it is."

Like most shops on the street, L&M had glass windows out front that let everyone passing by see what was inside. I could already see rows and rows of fabric, and I practically ran inside, with Ava right behind me.

"Can I help you?" A gray-haired woman wearing a dress with a colorful pattern approached us, looking over her skinny wire glasses.

"Um, yes," I said, taking the sketch out of my bag. "I'm looking for a silky gray fabric for this dress, plus some pink satin for the lining."

The woman took the sketch from me and peered at it carefully.

"You did this?" she asked.

I nodded.

Then she smiled. "How lovely! Come follow me, sweetheart. I'll get you just what you need. My name's Miriam. I'm the M in the L and M Fabrics."

"I'm an M, too," I said. "I'm Mia, and this is Ava. It's nice to meet you."

Dad waved. "Did you forget about me? I'm the dad."

"Nice to meet you, Dad," Miriam said.

"We're taking a class at Parsons," I said. "And my mom told us to come here." I sometimes forget that in fashion, my mom is kind of famous.

When I told Miriam my mom's name, she said, "You're Sara's daughter?" And then she clapped her hands. "Must run in the family!"

Then she walked us all through the shop, which reminded me of a maze. The aisles twisted and turned, and I'm sure if we hadn't been with Miriam, we would have gotten lost.

She led us past plaids, florals, pinstripes, sequins, and satins. First, she stopped at a roll of thin, gray fabric with a slight shimmer.

"It's exactly what I had imagined!" I said, feeling the smooth fabric between my fingers.

Then we were off again, and she helped me find the perfect shade of pink satin. We took the rolls to the fabric cutting table, and Miriam asked me questions about the measurements of the dress and calculated how much fabric I would need (with extra to account for mistakes). Before long I was holding a neatly wrapped package of fabric, tied with a piece of string.

I couldn't help myself. I hugged her. "Miriam, you are the fairy godmother of fabric. Thank you so much."

She reached out and ruffled my hair. "And you are a sweetheart. You've raised a nice girl here, Dad."

"I know," Dad said, and I'm sure I blushed.

Then he looked at his watch. "Okay, back to the subway! I've got to get you two girls to your class."

We left L&M Fabrics and went back to Parsons. (It's officially called Parsons The New School for Design, but it's easier to just say Parsons.) It's one of the top fashion design schools in the country—maybe even the world—and even though I'm not in college, they offer workshops for kids on the weekends.

The class is held every Saturday, but I go every other week, and they said that was okay when I signed up. Basically, it's like an open workshop where you can work on your own projects, and design students will help you with them.

The school is this tall, cool-looking building with long, glass windows going all the way up. Dad dropped off Ava and me by the front entrance.

"See you at one," he said, and I gave him a kiss on the cheek.

"Thanks for the fabric," I said, and Dad smiled.

"Anything for *mija*," he said, using his pet name for me. Then he waved, and Ava and I walked through the front doors.

"I can't believe you're going to sew that dress," Ava was saying as we headed to our workroom. "I'm still trying to get the pockets right on that denim skirt I started three weeks ago."

"And it's going to be adorable when it's done," I told her. "But I have to do something ambitious for the contest. Can you believe Katie told me the dress was boring? We had, like, kind of a big fight over it."

Ava stopped and looked at me, surprised. "I didn't think you and Katie ever fought."

"Well, she insulted my dress, and then I asked Emma and Alexis if they wanted to model it, and then Katie got all mad because I didn't ask her, too," I explained. "I mean, why would I ask her to model a dress that she doesn't even like?"

Ava shook her head. "She's crazy if she doesn't like it. It's gorgeous, and you are so going to win!" she assured me as we pushed open the workroom doors.

"Hey! It's a Mia week!" a cheerful voice said, and I looked up to see one of the design students, Millicent, standing there.

I totally adore Millicent. She's twenty-one and has this perfect caramel skin and curly black hair that she sometimes puts up in all these crazy ponytails. And every time I see her, I'm surprised by what she's wearing.

This morning, she had on hot-pink-and-black–striped tights, a pink tutulike skirt, a fitted black tank top, and a short white cardigan over it. She had her hair in two puffy ponytails on top of her head, with a pink ribbon tied around one of them.

"Tokyo street fashion?" I guessed, and Millicent smiled and nodded.

"I had sushi last night, and it got me in a Japanese mood," she said. "So, what are you working on today?"

"I'm finishing those pockets!" Ava said, emptying her backpack onto one of the worktables as some of the other students started streaming in.

"Actually, I really need your help," I told Millicent. She motioned me to follow her to an empty table, and I laid my package of fabric on top. Then I took out my sketch to show her.

"I'm entering this design contest," I said. "It's my fantasy dress. What do you think?"

Millicent picked up the sketch. "Wow, Mia!" she said. "This is really sophisticated. And you're lining

38

it with satin? That won't be easy to do."

"I know," I said, opening my package. "But I got the fabric, and it's so beautiful, I just have to use it."

Millicent felt the fabric between her fingers. "Yeah, I get it," she said. "Okay, so first things first. You know what measurements you want?"

I nodded. "Yeah, my friend Emma is going to model it for me."

"Then let's get you started on a pattern," she said. "It's going to seem like a really big deal to make this dress, but if you just take it one step at a time, you'll be fine."

I took a deep breath. "Okay. Let's do this!"

With Millicent guiding me through it, I felt pretty confident making the pattern. I used this really thin paper and draped it over a dress form that basically had the same measurements as Emma. Millicent reminded me to leave enough room for seams as I cut out the pattern.

By the time one o'clock came around, I had all the pattern pieces cut out. Millicent high-fived me.

"Nice job, Mia," she said. "You're going to do great."

"Thanks," I said.

"Hey, check it out!"

I turned to see Ava behind me. She had changed

out of her jeans and was wearing a totally cute denim skirt, with her hands stuffed into the front pockets.

"Pockets!" she said proudly.

"Ava, it's adorable!" I cried.

"Thanks," she said. "Did you get your pattern done?"

I nodded. "Millicent helped me."

Then we packed up our stuff, said good-bye to Millicent, and headed outside. Dad took us to Mega Burger for lunch, and then we walked past this shop that sold cute tights, and I bought a pair just like Millicent's. It was a perfect day.

Well, almost perfect. Because all day long, in the back of my mind, I knew Katie was still mad at me, and that didn't feel so good.

CHAPTER 5

What Was I Thinking?

That night I carefully opened up my material onto the sewing table in my room in Dad's apartment. When I started taking the class, he bought me the table and a sewing machine, so I could work on projects when I was there.

I stared at the fabric, still not quite believing how perfect it was. It seemed almost a shame to cut into it, but I knew I would have to. Then I remembered something. In class, Millicent is always saying we should first do a rough version of our patterns in muslin. Muslin is a thin, white fabric. You use your pattern to cut pieces out of muslin and roughly sew them together. That way, you can see if the fit is right before you cut into your expensive fabric.

"I should have asked Miriam for some muslin,"

I muttered, frowning, but then I started wondering if I had time to do the muslin thing. When was the contest deadline, anyway?

I rummaged in my bag for my copy of *Teen Runway* magazine and turned to the ad for the contest. Where was the deadline? Then I found it, in tiny print.

All entries must be postmarked by November 3.

November 3? Even if I used overnight mail to send in the photo of Emma wearing the dress, that only gave me a little more than a week to sew the dress! I definitely didn't have time to do a rough muslin version.

"Nooooo!" I wailed.

Dad appeared in my doorway. "Everything okay, *mija*?"

I sighed. "I just realized I only have, like, a week to sew the dress," I said. "That's impossible!"

"That doesn't sound like the Mia I know," Dad said. "On those shows you make me watch, don't they sew beautiful gowns in one day? If they can do that, then you can do it in a week."

"But they're all professional designers," I protested. "I'm just learning!"

Dad nodded. "That's true. But you're also very talented. You should at least give it a try. What have you got to lose? If you don't finish in time, you'll at least have a beautiful dress."

"I guess you're right," I admitted. "If I want this badly enough, I've got to try. But that means I need to cut my fabric tonight. We can't watch a movie together."

Dad put his two hands over his heart. "My heart is breaking, but I will get over it," he teased. "Can I help you?"

I thought about it. "No, I think I've got it. I can start sewing tomorrow when I get back to Mom's. Except I have a Cupcake Club meeting tomorrow night. *Argh!* I'm never going to be able to do this!"

"Deep breaths, *mija*," Dad told me. "You can take an earlier train. Then you'll have all afternoon to sew. You did your homework after lunch, right?"

"All done," I assured him.

"See? It's going to be fine."

I got up and gave him a hug. Dad always knew how to make me feel better. Sometimes I still wish it could be like it used to be, when I saw him every day.

"Thanks," I said. "Now I'd better get down to business."

Cutting out the pieces of fabric from the pattern was more difficult than it sounded. First, I had to iron the fabric and then pin each pattern piece to it. I worked on the gray fabric first, and then the pink. At first, I was sweating a little every time I cut into the fabric. What if I messed up? But when I was done, I had all my finished pieces perfectly stacked.

Dad came back into my room just as I was cleaning up. "It's really late, Mia. You should get some sleep."

"I got a lot done," I told him. "I think I can do this."

He smiled at me. "I know you can!"

On the train home the next morning, I had two things on my mind:

1. How was I going to finish the dress?
2. Was it going to be weird to see Katie that night at the Cupcake Club meeting?

I didn't know how to handle number two yet, but I decided I could tackle problem number one with some Alexis-style scheduling. I divided a page of my sketchbook into ten squares—the number of days I had to finish. Then I figured out how much sewing I needed to do each day, adding in my Cupcake Club meetings that I remembered. If I stuck to the schedule, I could have the dress done by next Sunday, do a fitting with Emma, make adjustments, and then take the final photo.

"Whew!" I said out loud, looking at it. It would be tough, but I could do it.

I told my mom my plan when she picked me up at the train station.

"My homework is done, so I'm going to sew all afternoon until the Cupcake Club meeting," I said, and then I frowned.

"What's wrong?" Mom asked.

"I had a big fight with Katie," I said, and it felt good to get it out. "She said she didn't like my sketch for the dress! She actually called it boring!" I told Mom the rest of the story, including how I had tried to explain myself to Katie but made it worse by calling her Silly Arms.

"Hmm," Mom said. "Well, Mia, it sounds like your feelings were hurt by Katie's comments, and you may have lashed out a bit."

"Well, yeah," I admitted. "But, I mean, what does she know about fashion anyway?"

We pulled up at a traffic light, and Mom looked at me. "Let me give you some advice. If you are to become a fashion designer, you have to learn two very important things: one is how to talk to people, especially potential clients. The other, is how to take criticism."

"But if I'm proud of my work, shouldn't I defend it?" I asked.

"It's all in the way you do it," Mom said. "First of all, remember that everyone has different tastes. What you may think is classic and chic, someone else may think is plain or dull. Something you may think is overworked and over-the-top might look gorgeous to someone else. So when somebody expresses his or her opinion, don't take it personally. And remember that everyone has his or her own style. That's what makes things interesting."

I thought about that. Katie loves everything rainbow colored; we sometimes joke that her bedroom looks like a unicorn threw up in it. It made sense that she wouldn't like my gray dress.

"Besides, friends are more important than fashion," Mom went on. "I'd hate to think of you fighting with Katie over a dress, of all things."

It was like my being mad at Katie was a balloon, and Mom popped it. Suddenly, I didn't even feel mad or annoyed with her anymore—I just felt terrible about what I had said to her.

I got out my phone and texted Katie.

See you tonight! ☺

    I waited, hoping she would text me back right away, but she didn't. That made me nervous.
What if Katie could never forgive me?

CHAPTER 6

Rainbows and Cupcakes

$\mathcal{I}$ was kind of glad that I had so much sewing to do, because it kept my mind off Katie all afternoon. Before I knew it, Mom was calling me down to dinner (Eddie's roast chicken and Mom's rice and peas). Then Mom drove me to Alexis's house for our Sunday night Cupcake Club meeting.

I was really nervous as I rang the bell. What if Katie wasn't talking to me? How would we bake cupcakes together? It would be so awkward and terrible.

Then the door opened, and Katie was standing there.

"I'm sorry!" we both said at the same time, and then we started laughing, crying, and apologizing all at once.

"I should never have criticized your dress. You're the fashion expert!"

"I was wrong to get mad when you said the dress was plain. It *is* plain, and I know you love bright colors."

"But I shouldn't have said it was boring . . ."

"And I shouldn't have called you Silly Arms . . ."

"Let's promise never to fight again!"

"Never, ever again!"

Alexis stepped in between us. "Okay! Enough with the lovefest!" she teased. "Can we please get back to business as usual now?"

I hugged Katie one more time. "Okay, now we can!"

We followed Alexis into her kitchen, where Emma was filling the cupcake pans with paper cups. Alexis's kitchen is superneat, and Alexis had all the baking ingredients set out in a row on the counter. I took the bag of decorating supplies I had brought and dumped it out onto the kitchen table. Alexis grimaced.

"Sorry about the mess," I said. "It's just . . . we have so many ideas to test out, so I brought a lot of stuff."

The table was covered with small tubes of decorating gel, bags of skinny black licorice, jelly beans in Halloween colors—black, green, orange, and purple—and other small bags of candy that I thought would be interesting. Mom had also picked up some candy eyeballs for us. They're pretty easy to find in the baking section of the craft store.

"I thought for the test batch we should do the pumpkin cupcakes, since we can make vanilla and chocolate ones in our sleep," Alexis said.

Katie held up a can of puréed pumpkin. "I brought the stuff."

"And I've got butter softening for the icing," Emma said, nodding to her pink stand mixer, which she had brought for our baking session. "I figure we can do vanilla and then try a bunch of different colors."

"I'll get to work on the batter," Katie said.

"I'll help," I offered.

While Emma and Alexis worked on the icing, I helped Katie make the pumpkin cupcakes. She told me what she needed, and I measured it out for her: flour, eggs, cinnamon, nutmeg, pumpkin. . . . There were a lot of ingredients. When the batter was done, we poured it into the cups and then put it in the oven to bake. That gave us about twenty minutes to clean up and hang out.

"So, I can't believe George's party is this coming Saturday!" Emma said. "I think I know what my costume's going to be. My mom's helping me with it."

"Ooh, what are you going to be?" Katie asked.

Emma's eyes twinkled. "I kind of want it to be a surprise."

"Well, I don't mind telling you all my costume—" Alexis began, but Emma raised her hand.

"No, don't!" she cried. "I mean, we do everything together. We have a business together, we study together, we hang out together. Which is great. So maybe just this once we should surprise one another."

"Cool!" Katie said. "I am definitely going to surprise you guys."

"Yeah, sure," I agreed, but inside, I was thinking, *My surprise might be that I don't have a costume!* It was the last thing on my mind, really.

Alexis dried her hands on a dish towel. "We should do some scheduling. George's party is Saturday night, so we can't bake then. So when do we want to do the cupcakes for Angelo Ricco's party?"

"Saturday morning?" Katie asked.

"Or we could bake Friday night and decorate

51

Saturday morning," Emma suggested. "It's always easier to decorate when the cupcakes are cool."

My mind was racing. Friday night. Saturday morning. When would I find time to sew?

"Um, would you guys mind if I skipped baking Friday night?" I asked. "I only have a week to sew the dress for the contest and . . ."

"Of course!" Katie said quickly. "But you can decorate Saturday morning, right? I mean, we really need you for that."

I nodded. I'd make it work somehow. "Sure."

"That works for me," Alexis said. "And that will give us time to get ready for the party that night."

The timer went off, and Alexis took the cupcakes out of the oven. Katie did that trick where you stick a toothpick in the center, and if it comes up clean, it means the cupcakes are done. Then we put them in the fridge to cool off quickly, because if you put icing on warm cupcakes, it will just be a melted mess.

We started talking about George's party again.

"So, Katie, are you and George going to his party together?" Alexis asked.

"Well, George will already be there, so it's not like we can go together," Katie said.

"You know what I mean," Alexis said. "Are you

going together, like hanging out at the party as a couple?"

Katie's cheeks turned pink, and she shrugged. "Not really. It's not like a school dance or something. And it's not like he asked me. Why, are you *going* with Matt?"

Matt is Emma's brother, who's a grade above us. Sometimes it seems like he and Alexis are all flirty with each other, and other times they're just friends. It's sometimes really weird for Emma to be in the middle.

Now Alexis's cheeks turned pink. "Well, George only invited kids from our grade, so Matt's not going." Then she looked at me. "What about you and Chris?"

I'm pretty sure Chris likes me, because we have gone to stuff together, like the pep rally parade. I'd been so busy working on the dress that it hadn't occurred to me that Chris hadn't asked me to go to the party with him yet.

"Um, I don't know," I answered, suddenly feeling uncomfortable. "I haven't talked to him much lately."

"Well, the party's still a week away," Katie said. "Maybe he's just waiting to ask you."

I shrugged. "There's no rule that says he has to

ask me to go with him. As long as we're both there, right?"

"Of course," Emma assured me, only I wasn't feeling so assured. It *was* kind of weird that Chris hadn't asked me yet.

Katie opened the fridge and poked one of the cupcakes. "They're good," she said. "Let's get decorating."

"We should taste test one without icing first, to see how the pumpkin flavor came out," Alexis suggested.

"Good idea," Katie agreed. She cut one of the cupcakes into four pieces, and we each took a bite.

"Mmm, pumpkiny!" Emma said.

"Yes, the pumpkin flavor is nice," Katie said thoughtfully. "It might just need a pinch more cinnamon, though."

I looked at the bowls of icing that Emma and Alexis had made: lime green, orange, purple, and dark chocolate brown.

"So, let's do, like, four cupcakes in each color," I suggested. "Then we can try different techniques on each."

Katie raised her hand. "I call purple!"

A few minutes later we had the whole batch iced, and I quickly forgot about my dress and Chris while we experimented with the decorations. First, I took a chocolate-iced cupcake and stuck four pieces of licorice on each side to make spider legs. Then I added candy eyeballs.

"Hmm," I mused, standing back. "It still needs something."

"Sprinkles!" Katie said, handing me a small jar of chocolate sprinkles. "That will make the body look nice and fuzzy, like a tarantula."

I carefully applied sprinkles to the top of the cupcake. "You're a genius!" I cried. "This looks great."

Katie grinned. "I learned from the best."

Emma held up a cupcake with purple icing. She had made a monster face with jelly bean eyes and a gel-icing mouth with candy-corn teeth.

"That is so cute!" Katie cried. "Now I want to make a monster, too!"

I took a cupcake with lime green icing and stared at it. Then I picked up six round fruit candies in different colors and put them on top to look like eyeballs. I used a gel-icing pen to draw a black dot inside each "eye." Then I picked up a skinny length of red licorice, cut off a short piece, and shaped it into a grimace on the monster's face. A jelly bean made the perfect tongue.

"The kids are going to love these monster cupcakes," Alexis said. "Perfect. We'll need to take pictures of the cupcakes we make for the party and add them to our website. I'll bet we get a lot more Halloween bookings next year."

"Good idea," I said. I wiped off my hands and took out my phone. "Let me take some pictures now, so that we can remember what we did when we make them for real next week."

Then I yawned. It had been a really long weekend.

"Mia! You just made me yawn too!" Katie said, covering her mouth.

"Yawns are contagious," Emma said, yawning. "It's a scientific fact."

"Is that really true?" Alexis asked, but then she broke into a yawn too. "Okay, maybe it is."

"Let's get everything cleaned up," Katie said. "Suddenly, I can't stop thinking about my comfy bed."

I took pictures of our designs, and then we all cleaned up the kitchen. I texted Mom, and she came to pick me up a few minutes later.

"So, did you and Katie work things out?" she asked.

"Yes!" I replied. "Right away."

Mom smiled. "That's nice, Mia. And it makes me happy."

"Me too," I said. "But I'll be happier when my dress is done and all these Halloween parties are over. I don't know how I'm going to do it all!"

"Just take it one day at a time, Mia," Mom said. "Then it won't seem like such a big mountain to climb."

"I guess," I said, leaning back in my seat, but I wasn't sure if it was going to be so easy.

I didn't know it yet, but some things were going to be easier than I thought—and some things were going to be a lot harder.

CHAPTER 7

If I Could Go Back in Time . . .

So, in the week leading up to George's party, I did two pretty dumb things. I hate to use that word, but I still look back on that week and think, *You know, you really could have done that differently, Mia. That was really dumb.*

But I should start at the beginning. The day after our cupcake test was a Monday, and it ended up being a pretty regular day. As soon as I got home from school, I did all my homework, which took me two long hours. I started sewing right away, but by the time I threaded my sewing machine and lined up my seams with the needle, Mom was calling me for dinner.

At the table, I started shoveling chicken breast and sautéed broccoli into my mouth even faster than Dan usually does. Eddie raised an eyebrow.

"Where's the fire, Mia?" he asked.

I dropped my fork. "Fire? What fire?"

Eddie chuckled. "Sorry, it's an expression. You're eating so fast, I thought maybe you were hurrying to put out a fire somewhere."

"Well, I guess it's like a metaphor," I said, channeling my English homework. "Finishing this dress is like putting out a fire, because I have to get it done really fast."

"Actually, that's a simile," Dan said, with a mouth full of chicken, and we all stared at him.

He shrugged. "What? She used 'like' to compare the two things. Just because I play basketball doesn't mean I don't know what a simile is!" Everybody laughed.

"Point taken," Eddie said. "And, Mia, I understand what you mean."

"Just take it slow," Mom advised. "If you go too fast, you'll make mistakes."

"But I *have* to go fast, or I won't get it done," I said, standing up from the table. "Anyway, if you let me stay up an hour later each night, then I could go slower, and—"

"No," Mom interrupted, shaking her head. "Sleep is important, Mia. And I really don't want this contest to affect your schoolwork."

"But I'm getting all my homework done after school!" I protested.

"I know, but you also need to be awake and alert during the day," Mom said. "And if I let you stay up late, you'll be too tired to focus."

I sighed. I knew it was no use arguing with Mom.

"Fine," I said. "But if I don't get my dress done on time, it will be your fault!"

I stomped upstairs, angry, even though deep down I knew it wouldn't be Mom's fault at all. I was just freaking out about the whole thing, and I guess I wasn't being very rational. Then I sat down at my machine and started sewing, and right away the satin lining started to bunch. Frustrated, I had to carefully pull out the stitches and then try again.

"Deep breaths, Mia."

I looked up to see Mom in the doorway. Even though I had just acted like a jerk to her, she had a kind expression on her face.

"I know this is stressful for you, sweetheart," she said. "Just take it slowly, okay?"

"I know you're right," I admitted. "It's just so hard. I don't have enough time to get everything done."

"Well, I'm here if you need help," Mom said, and that made me feel better.

I took her advice and really tried to slow down. It paid off, because by the time I was supposed to go to bed, I had finished the cape for the dress. I put it over my shoulders and modeled it in my mirror.

"Gorgeous!" I said, and I started to feel excited about the contest again. I just *knew* I was going to win. . . .

And then Tuesday night, I was sure I was going to lose. I followed the same schedule: school, homework, dinner, sewing. I took deep breaths and did things slowly. But I was working on the long dress, and that wasn't quite as easy as the cape.

My biggest problem ended up being the slit going up the side of the dress. I wasn't sure how to finish the seams with the lining so that you couldn't see the stitches when the lining showed. It was really tricky. Mom came in and showed me how to do it, and even though I kind of got the hang of it, it didn't look as perfect as I wanted it to. *And* I was behind schedule.

I leaned back in my chair, looking at all the fabric piled around me, and the cut threads dangling everywhere, and the disorganized fabric pieces splayed out on my bed.

"This is a recipe for disaster!" I cried, but there was nothing I could do about it. I had to be in bed in five minutes, and I was so tired, I didn't want to stay up anyway.

The next day at school, all I could think about was the dress. In math class I tuned out Mr. K.'s voice until it sounded like bees buzzing in the background. In English class, we were supposed to be reading, but I just kept sketching my dress over and over again. And when we played basketball in gym, I wasn't paying attention when Katie passed me the ball, and it hit me right on the head!

"Oh my gosh, Mia. I'm so sorry!" she cried, running toward me as the ball bounced out-of-bounds.

"It's not your fault," I told her. "All I can think about is my dress. I'm not concentrating on anything!"

"Well, all I can think about is Halloween," Katie said. "The basketball reminded me of a pumpkin, and I kept thinking about the jack-o'-lanterns Mom and I are going to carve tonight. I should have been more careful with my throw."

"I'm fine, I swear!" I told her. "Maybe it will clear my head."

But it didn't. In fact, right after gym is when I did those two really not-so-smart things.

You see, we're not supposed to text in school, but nobody bothers you if you do it during lunch. So as soon as I sat down, I took out my phone and started texting Millicent.

It's Mia from class. Having so much trouble with the side slit on my dress. Help!

Millicent texted me right back.

Walk me through it. What's happening?

I was so grateful for Millicent's help that I once again tuned out everything that was going on around me. Katie, Emma, and Alexis were talking about George's party, but that was the last thing on my mind.

Then a voice cut through the chatter.

"Hey, Mia."

I kept one eye on the phone, still texting, and looked up with the other eye. Chris was standing there.

"Hi," I said, my fingers still tapping on the screen.

"So, um, I sent you a text last night. Did you get it?"

"Oh. A text? Last night? I'm not sure." Actually, I

had heard a few texts come in last night, but I didn't check them. I didn't want to stop working on the dress.

"Well, see, I wanted to ask you something," Chris said.

Now, if I could go back in time, I would march right up to myself at this moment and say, *Mia, put down the phone! Chris is about to ask you something important! And he's wearing that cute striped shirt that brings out the green in his eyes! If you don't put down that phone right now, you will totally regret it!*

But obviously time travel does not exist, because no future Mia showed up to save me from what happened next.

"Chris, could I talk to you later?" I asked, looking at the screen. "I'm right in the middle of something."

"Um, yeah, sure," Chris said, and if I had been looking at him, I probably would have seen how hurt he looked as he walked away.

When I finally put down the phone, I saw that Katie, Emma, and Alexis were all staring at me.

"What?" I asked.

"Um, did you just totally blow off Chris on purpose?" Katie asked.

"What do you mean?" I protested. "I didn't

blow him off. I was polite and said I would talk to him later."

"That's not exactly how it came across," Alexis said.

I sighed. "Listen, I can't worry about every little word that comes out of my mouth right now. I have got to finish this dress!" I said. "Which reminds me, Emma—could we do a dress fitting on Sunday night? I should be done by then. That would give me just enough time to make alterations before we photograph you in it."

Emma shook her head. "Sorry. Sunday night we're going to my aunt's for my cousin's birthday. Maybe Saturday?"

I bit my lower lip. No way would I be done by Saturday.

"Ummmmm . . . I don't know. Let me think. I was planning on sewing all Saturday afternoon, after we finish the cupcakes for Angelo Ricco's party."

Then Emma got an excited look on her face. "I know! We're really good friends with the Riccos. I bet Mrs. Ricco would let us do it there."

"At the party?" I asked.

"After we set up. We could go into one of the bedrooms or something," Emma said. "I'll ask her."

Once again, if I had a time machine, I might

have interrupted myself and stopped Emma here.

Hey, maybe bringing a fancy dress to a kid's party isn't the best idea, I would say, and then Emma and I would think of something else.

But that never happened. Instead, I told Emma that would be fine.

Because what could go wrong, right?

How about . . . *everything*!

CHAPTER 8

He Said What?

The next two days were a blur of school, homework, sewing; school, homework, sewing . . . Luckily, I had Mom to help me with problems, and Millicent answered every single text I sent her. She is amazing.

On Friday night, Mom and Eddie even let me stay up until midnight. I was glad at the time, but when my alarm went off at eight the next morning, I groaned.

"Nooooo!"

I turned off the alarm and pulled my pillow over my face. I didn't want to get up. But I had to be at Emma's at nine to decorate the cupcakes, and I didn't want to let down my friends—especially since they had done the baking without me last night.

Still grumbling, I climbed out of bed and made my way to the bathroom. A few minutes later I was downstairs, wearing leggings and a T-shirt and with my hair pulled back into a ponytail. I grabbed a box of cereal from the cabinet and walked over to the kitchen table, yawning. Mom and Eddie were sitting there, drinking coffee.

"Late night last night?" Eddie teased.

"I'm fine," I said. I didn't want them to think I couldn't handle staying up late.

"Well, I'll be glad when your deadline arrives and you can go back to your regular schedule, Mia," Mom said. "Although it's nice to see you working hard at something."

"Thanks," I said. "Can you give me a ride to Emma's? I've got to be there by nine."

"Sure," Mom said. "Remind me of your schedule again? You've got a bunch of parties this weekend, right?"

"George's party is tonight, and tomorrow we're delivering cupcakes to a little kid's party in the afternoon," I said. "I'm going to be sewing the rest of the time."

"And doing homework," Mom added.

I rolled my eyes. "Yeeeees. When have I ever not done my homework?"

"Just making sure," Mom said.

Since I was so close to my deadline, it was hard to break away from my sewing to decorate cupcakes. But when I got to Emma's house, I immediately started to relax.

"Mia! You're here!" Katie squealed when she answered the door. "We missed you last night!"

She pulled me inside the house and into Emma's kitchen. Music was blasting from speakers on the counter. Emma was mixing a batch of icing, Alexis was neatly pouring candy into small bowls, and Emma's little brother, Jake, was building something out of tiny plastic blocks on the kitchen table.

Emma turned off the mixer. "Hey!" she called out. "Mom's working and Dad had to drive Sam to SAT practice or something, so we're unsupervised." She waggled her eyebrows and giggled.

"Isn't Matt technically in charge, since he's the oldest one in the house right now?" Alexis asked.

Emma snorted. "Matt is sleeping, and, anyway, I am way more mature than he is," she replied. "In any case, since we don't need the oven today, Dad was okay with leaving us."

"Well, one day we'll have our own bakery, and we'll be supervising ourselves, anyway," Katie pointed out.

"Wait, how can I run a bakery and be a fashion designer at the same time?" I asked.

"Haven't you heard of multitasking?" Katie asked. She nodded to Alexis. "It's good to have more than one way to make money, right?"

"Multiple income streams," Alexis answered with a nod. "Although it might make more sense if the businesses were related. Like, Mia could design a line of aprons or chef whites."

I made a face. "I was kind of thinking of something more glamorous."

"No, it's a great idea!" Katie said, her eyes shining. "You would design the most adorable aprons! I bet we could sell millions."

"You know, I bet we could design our own aprons now if we wanted," Alexis said, making that face she always does when she's deep in thought. "There are lots of places online where you can do stuff like that."

I sat down on a chair. "Please, can I just get through this contest first before we start on the next thing? I'm exhausted!"

"Ooh, that's right. How's the dress going?" Emma asked.

"I finally feel like I can finish it," I said. "I'm pretty sure I can bring it to the party tomorrow for the fitting."

Emma clapped her hands together. "I can't wait!"

Then Alexis started talking in her let's-get-down-to-business voice. "So, we have four dozen cupcakes to decorate. We'll meet at the Riccos' house tomorrow at one to set up. Mia, I knew you were busy, so I got a Halloween tablecloth and some cobwebby stuff to put around our display."

I nodded. "Thanks. If I can think of anything fun to add, I will."

"So, I asked Mrs. Ricco if I could try on the dress tomorrow, and she said okay," Emma said. "She was hoping that we would stay and help with the kids and serving the food. She's going to pay extra, and it's only for, like, an hour or so. She says she has all the games and stuff."

Alexis opened her notebook. "I'll add it to her invoice. You told her our rates?"

Emma nodded. "Yes. She was cool with it."

"Excellent!" Alexis said. "We'll be over our earnings projections for next month."

"I'm not sure what that means, but it sounds good," said Katie.

Alexis smiled. "It is."

Emma spooned a big glob of orange icing from

the mixer and put it in a bowl. "I think we can start decorating now."

"Yay!" Katie cried, picking up a tube of icing gel.

"So, we're doing a dozen monsters, a dozen spiders, a dozen tombstones, and a dozen jack-o'-lantern cupcakes," Alexis said.

"Let's ice the cupcakes for each batch and then put them on a pan, so we don't get confused," Emma suggested.

Katie nodded. "Then we can all do some of each kind."

With our plan in place, we began decorating the cupcakes. Jake became very interested.

"I want a monster!" he said after Katie made a monster cupcake.

"We'll see if we have extras at the end," Emma promised him. "And then you can make your own monster. How would you like that?"

Jake nodded. "With sharp fangs. And lots of eyes."

Jake is superadorable. I almost had a little stepbrother once. His name was Ethan, and his mom, Lynne, was dating my dad. Then they broke up, and I haven't seen them since. It was kind of weird. Ethan was annoying, but at times like these, I miss him a little.

I was thinking about this as I carefully poked spider legs into a cupcake when Emma's brother Matt came into the kitchen. He was wearing shorts and a basketball T-shirt, and his blond hair was all messed up, like he had just gotten out of bed. Which he had.

"Breakfast!" he cried, grabbing for a cupcake on the table.

Emma slapped his hand away. "No way! Wait until we're done, and if we have extra, then *maybe* you'll get one."

"Fine," Matt said. "I'll just have some cereal."

"That's probably a healthier breakfast for you, anyway," Alexis pointed out.

Matt turned to her. "So, what time are we going tonight?"

"Seven thirty," Alexis replied, and I looked at her, with my eyebrows raised.

"What?" she whispered. "I asked George if I could bring somebody, and he said okay."

"Oh . . . sure," I said. That was a pretty bold move on Alexis's part, but she made it sound like it wasn't such a big deal.

"I guess you're not going with Chris?" Emma asked me.

"Chris Howard?" Matt asked, and I nodded. "I

73

was talking to him yesterday. He said he wanted to ask you to go with him, but you were blowing him off."

I jumped out of my chair. "What? He said what?"

"He said you blew him off or something," Matt said with a shrug. He reached into the fridge and took out a carton of milk. "That's all I know."

"Maybe it has something to do with what happened in the cafeteria the other day," Katie carefully suggested.

I groaned. "You're probably right. I did kind of blow him off. And I never answered that text he sent me." I put my head in my hands. "Oh no. Now what do I do?"

"Text him right now!" Alexis suggested, and I did just that.

Hey, sorry I never got back to you, I typed quickly. Been really busy. How r u? R U going to George's party?

I hit send. Then I waited, hoping to get an instant response, but my phone was silent.

"He'll text you back," Katie said. "Just give him some time. Maybe he's still asleep or something."

"Yeah, he probably is," I agreed, and I went back to decorating cupcakes. Every time I finished a cupcake, I checked my phone. Nothing.

Pretty soon we had four dozen perfectly deco-rated cupcakes, six backups in case any got smooshed at the party, and six extras.

"One for each of us," Alexis said, handing them out. "And, Jake, you can make your own monster."

I checked my phone one last time. There was a message! I quickly grabbed it.

What time do I need to pick you up?

It was from Mom. I sighed.

"Look, a monster!" Jake held up his cupcake, which he had loaded with a mound of jelly beans, candy eyes, and candy corn.

Emma laughed. "That's more like a monster tummy ache," she said.

Come get me now? I typed back to Mom. It was only eleven thirty, and I still had plenty of time to sew.

I couldn't worry about Chris Howard right now. I had a dress to finish!

CHAPTER 9

Awkward with a Capital *A*

I went home, ate a quick sandwich, and got to work sewing. I was having a hard time with the seams on the bottom of the dress, and I had to take out the stitches and start again.

I was concentrating so hard on trying to finish the dress that I totally lost track of time. The next thing I knew, Mom was calling upstairs.

"Mia, Katie's here!"

"She's what?" I looked up from my machine and saw the red numbers on the digital clock: 6:30. "No!"

My heart started to pound. It couldn't be this late. Katie had texted me that she would come a little early so we could take pictures of our costumes. . . .

A costume! I had totally forgotten to get a

costume. I might have gone into a total panic if I hadn't been so tired. I sighed and turned off the machine.

"Send her up!" I called back.

Seconds later Katie bounded into my room.

"Ta-da!" she yelled.

She was wearing white chef's pants and a matching chef's jacket. Two brown braids stuck out from under a white chef's hat. In one hand she held a rubber chicken.

"Katie, you look adorable!" I cried, getting up to hug her.

"Thanks," she said, grinning. "It's so me, right?" Then she held up the rubber chicken. "And rubber chickens are always hilarious. I don't know why, but they just are."

"Totally!" I agreed. "I wish I had thought of a cool costume like that. I didn't even get one."

Katie held up a drawstring bag. "I thought maybe you were too busy to get a costume. So I brought mine from last year. It should fit you."

"You're so sweet!" I said, taking the bag from her. "What is it?"

"Just look," Katie said.

I opened the bag—and saw a bunch of white satin with big yellow, red, and blue polka dots.

77

"It's my clown costume, remember?" Katie asked. "It even comes with the red floppy shoes."

I pulled the costume out of the bag. The satin polka-dot pattern was a one-piece jumpsuit, with ruffles on the ends of the sleeves and pants. The long, floppy shoes were three times as big as my feet. I also pulled out a bright red nose made out of soft foam, and one of those Halloween makeup kits with white, red, and black stuff that you could put on your face.

"It's . . . wow," I said, searching for the right words. A fashion nightmare? Ridiculous? Hideous?

"I know it's not what you'd normally wear," Katie said. "But it's Halloween! It should be fun. And it's better than no costume at all, right?"

I had to think about it. What would be worse? Going to George's costume party with no costume or going in a horrible clown costume?

"George will crack up when he sees you," Katie prodded, and that helped me make up my mind. George is sweet and funny and nice, and I knew the party would be more fun if I wore a costume.

"Okay," I said. "But I am *not* wearing the nose."

I straightened up my fabric and then put on a shirt and shorts to wear under the costume. Then I thought of Millicent and put my hair in, like, eight crazy ponytails.

"That is awesome," Katie said. "But I still think you should wear the nose."

"I have another idea," I said. I opened up the makeup kit. The makeup came in tiny little plastic disks and was kind of thick, but I could make it work. "I can do kind of an artistic clown face, like a Harlequin."

Katie watched as I carefully applied a layer of white makeup all over my face. I patted that down with a tissue and then used the black on my lips and around my eyes. I painted big, exaggerated eyelashes coming down from the bottom of each eye, and then added a tiny black heart on my right cheek.

"Whoa, that is so cool," Katie said.

I leaned closer to the mirror. "Not bad," I agreed. "Now let me get on my floppy shoes so we can get out of here."

When we got downstairs, Katie's mom was sitting at the kitchen table with Mom and Eddie, talking. Mom let out a big gasp when she saw me.

"Mia! You look so cute!"

"It's thanks to Katie," I said. "She saved me with her clown costume."

Eddie jumped up. "You girls look wonderful! Let me take some pictures!"

79

We went into the living room, and Katie and I goofed around and did some funny poses with the rubber chicken—me pretending to kick it with my big shoe, Katie pretending to beat me over the head with it—and then Katie's mom drove us to the party.

It was easy to tell which house the party was at because Halloween music was blaring from speakers on the lawn. Fake tombstones rose up from the grass like jagged teeth, each one painted with a funny saying or name.

"Look, 'Barry M. Deep,'" Katie said, pointing, when we got out of the car. "And there's a baking one! 'Here Lies John Yeast. He'll Rise No More.' Ha! Get it?"

I shook my head, laughing. "I bet George did that one just for you."

We walked down the path to the front door, which was lined with glowing jack-o'-lanterns. It was a warm fall night, and the front door was wide open. George's living room was already packed with kids in costume. The lights were dimmed, and a green strobe light was flashing.

"Oh man, this is crazy!" Katie said happily as we stepped inside.

George pushed his way past a kid dressed as a

mummy and walked up to us. He was dressed like a hot dog: he wore a big stuffed hot dog in a bun, with mustard, over his shirt. On the bottom he wore jeans and sneakers.

"Katie! You're a chef! You can cook me!" he cried.

Katie waved the rubber chicken at him. "Hot dogs and chicken, mmm."

Then he looked at me. "Wow, is that you, Mia? Awesome. But where's your big red nose?"

"I told her she should wear it," Katie said.

"Hey, I'm in costume, right?" I pointed out. "And I don't see any other clowns here."

Most of the boys had opted for gory zombie costumes, with gross, bloody faces and torn clothes. And most of the girls wore cute costumes from the party store, with short, frilly skirts.

"Well, I'll *ketchup* to you later," George joked, pushing off into the crowd again.

"But you're wearing mustard!" Katie called after him, laughing.

"Oh my gosh, Mia!"

I spun around to see Alexis, Matt, and Emma standing there. Alexis had on a cute black dress and a black witch hat. Matt was dressed like a basketball player (which he is in real life). And Emma was an adorable fairy in a pink dress with a fluffy organza skirt, glittery white wings, and a fairy wand with an aluminum foil star at the top.

"You look amazing!" Emma said. "I love your makeup."

"Thanks!" I said. "Katie hooked me up with a costume at the last minute. I know it's goofy, but—"

"It's supercute," Emma interrupted. "And nobody else here is wearing anything like it. But there are a dozen fairies here."

"You could start a fairy baseball team," Katie joked.

"And, anyway, your dress is really beautiful," I said.

Emma nodded. "Mona lent it to me," she said. Mona is a Cupcake customer who owns The Special Day bridal shop, where Emma models part-time. "It was a special-order bridesmaid's dress, and then the order was canceled. I got the cheapest wings at the costume store and put glitter on them, and Jake helped me make the wand."

"It's perfect!" Katie said. "How about you, Alexis?"

"Well, I borrowed this dress from Dylan, and I got the hat at the dollar store," Alexis said.

"Economical and chic," I told her, laughing.

Then her expression suddenly changed to a look of unhappy surprise.

"Alexis, what's wrong?" I asked.

"Um, well, Chris is here," she said.

I turned and followed her gaze to the front door, where Chris was walking in . . . with Talia Robinson. She's in a couple of my classes, but I don't really know her. I didn't think Chris knew her, either, but he obviously did, because it looked like he had come to the party with her.

Chris was dressed like the old-fashioned kind of vampire, with a red bow tie and black cape. Talia looked like a girl vampire with pale makeup, a black T-shirt, a short denim skirt, tights, and boots. Plastic fake fangs stuck out from her red lipstick. She looked totally cute.

I looked down at my polka-dotted clown suit and red, floppy shoes and wished I could sink into the floor. Chris had taken another girl to the party. Another girl! And she wasn't wearing a ridiculous clown costume, either.

Katie must have read my mind. "Maybe they're just walking in at the same time," she said.

But then George walked up to them and started talking to them, and I couldn't hear what they were saying, but they were all laughing, and then Chris kind of put his arm around Talia and led her over to the food table in the dining room.

"Unbelievable," Alexis said, and she sounded a little bit angry. "What is he doing here with her? He likes you."

"It's my fault," I said miserably. "Matt is right. I totally blew him off, and he took somebody else."

"He shouldn't have given up on you," Emma said. "He wouldn't have if he really liked you."

I looked at Matt. "What do you think?"

Matt shrugged. "Maybe Talia asked him, and he figured, why not? He could still like you."

Then the song "Monster Mash" came on over the speakers. Katie grabbed my hand.

"I love this song! We have to dance," she commanded.

"Dance? In this clown costume? I will trip over my own feet!" I protested.

"We'll all dance," Emma said, and I let Katie drag me into the middle of the room. She started doing this dance, where she waved the rubber chicken over her head, and then George came up and started break-dancing (which was impressive, considering he was wearing a hot dog costume). Then other people started joining us, like my friends Lucy and Sophie, and Eddie Rossi, who is taller than anybody in our grade, but he didn't look goofy at all when he danced.

Pretty soon I forgot about Chris and started having fun. Everyone was talking and dancing and hanging out. Then I got thirsty.

"I'm going to get some water," I told my friends, heading toward the dining room.

That's when my big clown feet bumped right into Chris! He turned around, and for a second he didn't recognize me. Then I saw him blush underneath his vampire makeup.

"Oh, hi, Mia," he said.

I looked behind him, but I didn't see Talia. "I thought you were here with Talia Robinson," I said, trying to sound like I didn't care, but I could hear my voice shaking.

"Well, yeah, I am, but uh . . . she's outside." Chris shifted back and forth on his feet. This whole situation was Awkward with a capital *A*.

I took a deep breath. "Listen," I said. "I'm sorry I didn't talk to you in the cafeteria the other day. I'm entering this big fashion design contest, and it's kept me busy for every second."

Chris nodded. "Yeah, okay." Then he kind of looked away from me. "I guess I thought you were just blowing me off."

"I didn't mean to," I said. I wanted to say, *I like you—why would I blow you off?* For some reason I couldn't bring myself to say the words. "Anyway, you could have asked me before you asked Talia."

"That's not what happened," Chris said. "It was— Whatever. I'm sorry if I hurt your feelings."

"Me too," I said, and then there was just awkward silence.

"Okay, then," I said finally. "Happy Halloween."

"You too," Chris said, and I grabbed a bottle of water and got out of there as fast as my floppy feet could carry me.

When I got back to the living room, Katie, Emma, and Alexis were all staring at me.

"What did he say?" Alexis asked.

"He said he was sorry," I reported. "It was kind of awkward. Can we just forget about it for now?"

"Of course," Katie said, grabbing my hand again. "George says he's bobbing for apples on the front lawn. I have got to see this!"

So I let Katie drag me out into the night, and because I was with my friends, and because Katie and George are hilarious, I had a good time, no matter what was happening with Chris.

And how lame is it to dress like a vampire, anyway? I mean, vampires are so last year!

CHAPTER 10

From Bad to Worse

After I washed off my makeup that night, I climbed into bed, exhausted. I was glad I was so tired. Otherwise, I might have had trouble sleeping, because my mind was full of thoughts about Chris and Talia, not to mention that the contest deadline was only days away.

I woke up groggy but with a weird energy coursing through me—it was now or never. I'd heard people use the expression "adrenalin rush"—when you're really nervous or excited and get a sudden burst of energy—but it had never happened to me personally. I had about three hours left to finish the dress before I had to head to Angelo Ricco's party with the Cupcake Club.

"Mia, you have to eat breakfast," Mom insisted

when she heard the sound of my sewing machine going.

"Can't eat. Have to finish," I told her.

"Mia," Mom said sternly, and I sighed and went downstairs. After a bowl of granola and a glass of OJ, I was back at work.

Finally, I finished the last seam. I carefully cut my thread and slid the dress out of the machine. I hung it on a hanger and put the cape over it.

"Not bad," I said, admiring my own work. I could see a few places where thread was hanging out, and the back zipper looked a tiny bit crooked, but I could probably fix that after the fitting.

Then I looked at the clock. It was only eleven! I had plenty of time to get ready.

I felt like a weight had been lifted off my shoulders. I took a long, hot shower and left the conditioner on my hair for a full three minutes, just like the bottle said. I properly blow-dried my hair and even used some shine oil on it. Then I put on my pink Cupcake Club T-shirt and my favorite pair of skinny jeans.

By the time Alexis's mom came by in her minivan to pick me up, I was feeling like myself again. Like the old, calm, confident Mia. I would go to the party and help out the Cupcake Club. I would enter the contest on time—and win! And then I would talk to Chris and see if he still liked me. I had a feeling that he did.

Mom had lent me a garment bag, so I could safely get the dress to the party. I carefully hung it up on a hook in the backseat of the minivan. Alexis, Emma, and Katie were already in the car, and our cupcakes and table decorations were stacked back in the hatch.

"Mia! I missed your face," Katie said when I climbed into the seat neat to her. "You didn't look like you with that makeup on last night."

Mrs. Becker turned and smiled at us. "Do you girls have everything? Are we set to go?"

"Check and check, Mom," Alexis told her, and then we drove to the Riccos' house.

The Riccos lived in a ranch-style house with a big, green front lawn covered with orange and yellow leaves and dotted with jack-o'-lanterns.

"It's like a regular pumpkin patch," Katie remarked as we made our way to the front door.

A woman dressed like a fortune-teller greeted us.

"Hi, Mrs. Ricco," Emma said.

"Emma! I'm so glad you're here," she said.

Emma introduced us. "This is Alexis, Katie, and Mia," she said. "We'll set up the cupcake table and then help you with whatever you need, okay?"

"Oh, I am so glad to see you girls," Mrs. Ricco said, motioning for us to follow her inside. "I've got the rest of the food set up, but I still need to fill all the goody bags. If you wouldn't mind helping me with that, I'd love it."

"No problem," Emma said. "It won't take us too long to set up the table."

Mrs. Ricco led us down to the bottom floor of the house, which was one big family room. Orange and black crepe-paper streamers looped down from the ceiling, and handmade paper ghosts decorated the walls.

She stopped in front of a small folding table in the corner. "Will this work?" she asked.

"It's perfect," replied Alexis. "We'll get started right away."

I was still holding the garment bag. "Um, Emma said it would be okay if she tried on the dress here, later. Is there someplace I can put it?"

"Oh, sure," Mrs. Ricco said. "I think it's so fantastic that you've designed your own dress. I can't wait to see it. Here, we can hang it up in the laundry room."

"Thanks," I said, following her, and soon the dress was safely hanging from a metal rack.

Then I got to work helping my friends. Alexis had bought two tablecloths, one orange and one black, and I folded them and draped them so that you could see both colors on the table. Then Katie set up the two round black tiers that we used to hold our cupcakes (we have two sets, white and black, and they manage to work for all kinds of events). I took some of the cobwebby stuff that Alexis had bought and piled it all around the tiers.

"Spooky!" Katie said, standing back to get a good look.

"And now, the cupcakes," Emma said, holding up the carrier. "I think we should put a mix on each tier."

"Good idea," Alexis agreed.

Mrs. Ricco came over to watch. "Oh my gosh, these look yummy!" she said. "I just have to taste one."

Alexis handed her a jack-o'-lantern cupcake. "This one is pumpkin, our new flavor."

Mrs. Ricco didn't grab a napkin or anything. She ripped off the wrapper and bit right in.

"This is delicious," she said after her first bite. Then she walked toward the stairs. "Angelo! Come and see the delicious cupcakes these wonderful girls made for you."

Ten seconds later a little boy in a Spider-Man costume (without the mask) came bounding down the stairs.

"Cupcakes! Yay!" he said. Then he looked at Emma. "Where's Jake?"

"Hi, Angelo! He'll be here soon, when your party starts," Emma promised.

Then the doorbell rang. Mrs. Ricco sighed. "That must be my sister, Laura. She's always early. I'll be back down with the goody bag stuff!"

We set up the cupcakes neatly on the tiers and then got to work putting candy and Halloween stickers into the paper goody bags Mrs. Ricco had bought. When we were finished, I asked Emma if she could try on the dress before the party started.

"Oh, sure," Emma said. "I almost forgot."

She got her bag and then pulled a length of gray satin ribbon from it. "I was thinking that I'd use it to tie my hair back," she explained. "You know, to put more emphasis on the dress. I think it will match perfectly."

"That's a great idea," I said, glad Emma had thought of it. "And did you bring the shoes?"

When you're fitting a dress on a model, it's important she wears the shoes that go with it. The shoes you wear will affect the length of the dress, and I wanted to make sure everything was perfect.

Emma pulled out a pair of silver high heels. "Luckily, Mom and I are the same size."

"They're perfect!" I cried. "Come on, let's get you fitted."

We went into the laundry room, and Emma gasped happily when I unzipped the garment bag.

"Mia, it's beautiful!" she cried.

"Get changed and then call me, and I'll zip you up," I said, closing the door behind me.

On the floor above, I could hear the doorbell ring again, and some kids were starting to come down the stairs, followed by their parents. I felt bad doing the fitting while the party was going on, but I promised myself it wouldn't take long. Besides, I could see Alexis and Katie busily helping the kids with the cupcakes and snacks that Mrs. Ricco had put out.

Then I heard the laundry door open behind me, and I turned as Emma stepped out. She looked absolutely beautiful! The long, gray dress fit perfectly on her and made her look tall and glamorous.

The moms in the room came running up to us.

"What a beautiful dress!" said one.

"Isn't it amazing, Laura?" asked Mrs. Ricco. "I love the cape."

Another mom stepped up to Emma. "I wish I had somewhere to wear this," she said, looking at me. "I would hire you in a second to make me one just like it. In my size, of course."

You know that expression "beaming with pride"? Well, I must have been beaming like a lighthouse. The dress looked exactly how I'd hoped it would.

"It needs some adjustments in a few places," I said, taking out the pins, measuring tape, and notepad I had brought with me. "But once I'm done, it will be perfect."

"I love it, Mia," Emma said.

I had to tuck in the waist a bit, and lift up the hem about a quarter of an inch, but those changes wouldn't be too hard. I made a note of everything, and Alexis and Katie came over to admire the dress.

"Mind if I sit down?" Emma asked when I was done. "I'm not used to wearing these high heels. How do real models do it all day long?"

"If you were getting paid what a real model gets paid to wear those heels, trust me, you'd find a way," Alexis said with a laugh.

That's when one of the little girls in the room spotted Emma. She was dressed in a sparkly blue gown, with a crown on her head. She looked at

Emma, taking in her blond hair tied back with a shiny gray ribbon, her long gown, and shiny silver shoes, and burst out into a huge smile of excitement.

"Look, Mommy!" she cried, pointing at Emma. "She's a princess, just like me!"

"Hi, Isabella," Emma said, waving. She turned to us. "That's Isabella. She's Angelo's sister. Isn't she adorable?"

Then the adorable Isabella bolted across the room like a rocket and hurled herself into Emma's arms for a hug.

"Aw, how cuuuu—" Katie started to say, and then her faced changed to a mask of horror.

I was confused—until I saw the orange icing all over Isabella's fingers!

"Nooooo!" I wailed. Mrs. Ricco quickly scooped her off Emma.

"I'm so sorry," she said.

My heart was in my throat as I looked at Emma. Because the dress was strapless, and she wasn't wearing the cape, most of the icing was smeared on Emma's arms and neck. I was relieved for a second, and then I saw it. A thumbprint. One chubby orange thumbprint stamped right on the center of the neckline.

Mrs. Ricco ran up with a bottle of seltzer. "Try this, quick!" she said. "Seltzer gets out anything."

Alexis grabbed a napkin for me, and I soaked it in seltzer and dabbed it on the thumbprint. Now I had a *wet* orange thumbprint.

"Try salt," suggested Mrs. Ricco's sister, Laura. "You just rub a little in."

"I'll get some!" said Mrs. Ricco, and she came a minute later with a saltshaker. I rubbed some in, but it just left me with a salty, wet thumbprint.

"Maybe plain water will work?" Emma suggested, and we tried that, too. Nothing.

I sat down in one of the folding chairs, feeling numb. I could try to cover up the spot with the cape, but the spot was far away from where the cape would fit. The neckline was so simple and pretty, but now, with the spot . . .

"It's ruined," I said softly, tears stinging my eyes. Then I buried my head in my hands.

"Mia?"

I sniffled and looked up to see Katie standing in front of me. She was holding Emma's gray satin hair ribbon.

"I know you wanted to keep the dress plain, but I thought maybe you could use this as a trim along the neckline to hide the spot?" she said. "It's shiny, but it's the same shade of gray—exactly, just like Emma said."

I took the ribbon from Katie and held it up against the dress. The ribbon was an inch wide, just enough to cover the thumbprint but not too big to look out of place.

"Katie, you're a genius!" I shouted. "Quick, give me my pins!"

Alexis handed me my pins. "Don't move, Emma," I warned, and then I carefully pinned the ribbon in place, to see how it would look.

"It's even prettier than before," said Mrs. Ricco. "It adds just a nice little extra shimmer."

"Yes, it does," I agreed.

"Well, now that the crisis is averted, let's get back to work!" Alexis said in her businesslike way.

"Emma, please take off that princess dress immediately!" I ordered.

Emma hurried to the laundry room. "You got it!"

I turned to Katie. "Have I told you lately how awesome you are?"

"Yes," she said. "But I never get tired of hearing it!"

CHAPTER 11

Picture Perfect

𝒯he rest of the party went smoothly. The kids and parents loved the cupcakes, and Alexis even took a few holiday orders.

"So, Emma, can we do the photo shoot at my house tomorrow?" I asked. "Once I get it home, I'm not taking it anywhere until the pictures are taken."

Emma nodded. "Sure. Maybe, like, seven?"

"Perfect," I said. "And don't forget the shoes."

Emma groaned. "This heel thing might just break my modeling career."

I laughed. "I promise I won't keep you in them for too long."

When I got home, it was almost five o'clock. Mom walked out of her office.

"How did it go?" she asked.

"Well, the party went great," I said. "But I had a little problem with the dress." I told her all about Isabella and her orange icing hands—and how Katie had come up with the perfect solution.

Mom opened up the garment bag. "That ribbon does add a nice shine to the dress," she agreed. "Sewing it on might be tricky, so let me know if you need help, okay?"

"Thanks," I said. "I kind of need to get it done tonight. Emma is coming over tomorrow to take pictures."

Mom looked thoughtful. "Let me see if I can get some kind of backdrop for you. You want to make sure the dress is the focus of the photo, not what's in the background."

"Good idea," I said, and then I headed up the stairs.

"Mia?" Mom called out, and I looked back at her. "I'm really proud of you, you know."

I smiled. "Yeah, I know," I said. And then I went right up to my sewing machine.

"Does this look straight?" Eddie was asking.

It was Monday night, and thanks to Mom and Eddie, our living room had been transformed into a photo studio. One of Mom's friends at the Maple Grove Women's Club was a photographer, and Mom had borrowed a background stand and some seamless paper from her.

The stand is basically two tall metal poles on legs, with a metal pole that goes between them. Then you can hang fabric or whatever you're using for a backdrop on the top pole, and pull it down—kind of like a curtain. They use them at the photo studio in the mall where Mom used to take me to get my picture taken during the holidays when I was little.

Mom's friend had given her a big roll of white seamless paper, which is really straight and smooth when it hangs. Eddie had hooked the roll onto the top pole and was carefully pulling it down.

Katie had come over to help out with the shoot.

"It's good!" she told Eddie as he fussed with the paper. "What do you think, Mia?"

I stepped back to get a good look. "It works," I said, nodding.

Then Mom came downstairs with Emma, who was holding on to Mom's arm and carefully walking in her high heels. Since my mom's a professional stylist, I had asked her to help style Emma, and as usual Mom had made something look even more perfect. "Oh my gosh, you look gorgeous!" I cried when I saw Emma.

Mom had pulled back Emma's blond hair into a pretty, messy ponytail. I could see Katie looking at Emma's hair doubtfully.

"Don't worry, Katie," I assured her. "Messy is definitely *in*!"

Katie grinned. "Oh good! Because that's normally how my hair looks!"

Emma didn't look like she had makeup on, but up close I could see that Mom had added just a touch of light pink blush to her cheeks and pale pink gloss to her lips. Delicate silver earrings with a crystal dangling from each end sparkled whenever Emma moved.

"Mia, you sewed that ribbon on perfectly," Katie said, taking a closer look at the dress.

"Mom gave me some tips," I explained, smiling gratefully at my mom.

Eddie handed me his digital camera. "All right, Mia. Work your magic!"

I took a deep breath. I could have the best dress in the contest, but if I didn't have a great photo, it wouldn't matter.

"Okay," I said. "I'm allowed to submit four photos. So I'm thinking one with the cape, one without, one that shows the back, and one that features the slit in the skirt."

"Got it," Emma said, sounding very professional. She put on the cape and stepped in front of the white backdrop. Then she put her right foot forward a little bit. The slit opened up, revealing the pink satin lining.

"Perfect!" I said, and I started snapping pictures. "Okay, now one with your hands on your hips."

"Work it!" Katie called out, giggling, as Emma struck the pose.

"Emma, you really are a natural at this," my mom said, and Emma beamed. She really was. I could see why she kept getting modeling jobs.

"Keep smiling," I told her. "I want you to look like you're superhappy to be wearing the dress."

"Well, I am!" Emma said, flashing her dazzling smile.

I snapped a bunch of shots until I was sure I had enough to choose from.

"It's a wrap!" I called out.

Emma walked to the nearest chair and sat down. "Thank goodness!" she cried, taking off the shoes.

Eddie hooked the camera into a laptop he had set up in the living room. "Let's see what you've got before we take everything down."

I leaned over his shoulder, holding my breath as the photos loaded. Then they started popping up on the screen, one by one.

"Ooh, they came out great!" Emma cried.

"Beautiful dress, beautiful model, beautiful photos," said Mom. "You did such a wonderful job, Mia."

"If I print these out tonight, can you mail them for me while I'm in school?" I asked.

"Of course!" said Mom.

"Then what happens?" Katie asked.

I sighed. "Then . . . there's nothing to do but wait!"

CHAPTER 12

Manhattan Dreams

*T*hat night I checked the rules of the contest over and over again, but it didn't say anything about when the winners would be announced. How frustrating! I didn't even know if they would let me know by phone, or e-mail, or text, or regular mail.

Luckily, I had a weekend in Manhattan to distract me. When Dad picked me up from the train station, we had sushi, and then we went to an off-Broadway show featuring acrobats and music and flashing lights and stuff. The next day, I had my design class at Parsons.

Since the photos had been taken and were safely in the hands of the judges, I was a little less nervous about taking the dress out of my house. I had carefully packed it for the weekend, so I could show Millicent and Ava. I had packed copies of the photos, too.

Dad and I swung by to get Ava on the way to Parsons. Her eyes got big when she saw the garment bag I was carrying.

"Oh my gosh, did you finish?" she asked.

I nodded. "The deadline for the photos was Wednesday. I got done just in time."

"Let me see!" she pleaded.

"When we get to class," I promised. "I already had one near-disaster with this dress."

I told her about the cupcake incident on the way to class, and by the time we got to the workroom, she was practically jumping out of her boots.

"Millicent!" she cried, as soon as she spotted her. "Mia finished her dress!"

I could see Millicent was going for a street chic vibe that day, with a white boyfriend blazer over a black rock T-shirt, black leggings, and with low black boots. Her curls were wild and loose.

Millicent smiled when she saw us. "Cool. Let's check it out."

I hung up the garment bag on a clothing rack and carefully took out the dress.

"Nice, Mia," Millicent said, nodding approvingly. "Really good job with the lining."

"Thanks for all your help," I said. Then I took the photos out of my bag. "This is what it looks like on the model."

Ava peered over my shoulder to look. "Wow, Emma looks fabulous!" she cried. "Mia, this dress is amazing. You are so going to win the contest."

"You should be really proud of this," Millicent said. "Just remember that the fashion world is really competitive, so don't feel bad if you don't win. You've done great work here, and that's what matters."

I wasn't sure how to take what Millicent was saying. I couldn't imagine not winning. I suddenly felt worried.

"Do you think there will be a lot of dresses better than this?" I asked.

"'Better' is a tricky word," Millicent said. "One judge might think your dress is the best thing ever, but another might feel differently. It could all depend on what the judges like and don't like, and everybody's personal taste is different."

Ava nodded. "I know. When I watch those design shows on TV, sometimes I absolutely love a dress, and the judges hate it."

I knew Ava and Millicent were right, but I didn't want to think about it.

"Well, I need to stay positive," I said. "Winning

this contest could change my future."

"You're in control of your future, Mia, no matter what happens," Millicent said. "You'll still want to go to design school, even if you win, right?"

I hadn't really thought it through, but it made sense. "Sure."

"So winning would be nice, but it wouldn't really change anything," Millicent said. "And if you go to school here, you can work with up-and-coming designers on Saturdays. You meet some pretty cool people doing that."

I hugged her. "You're the best. Thanks! And I would so love to come here."

"Me too," added Ava. "Won't that be amazing? We can get our own apartment and be roommates and go to classes together!"

"Definitely!" I agreed. "It seems so far away, but it really isn't. Is it?"

"It goes fast," Millicent assured us. She looked at her watch. "Just like this class. Let's get sewing!"

The rest of the weekend was full of plenty of things to distract me from the contest. I went to Ava's Saturday afternoon soccer game and watched scary movies with Dad. And on Sunday, Katie had invited me over to hang out when I got back from Manhattan.

When my mom dropped me off at Katie's, I was surprised to see Mr. Green there with Katie's mom. I usually only ever see Mr. Green in school, and it's weird to see him anywhere else—especially Katie's house. Mrs. Brown was carrying one of those old-fashioned wicker picnic baskets.

"Hi, Mia," she said. "It's such a beautiful fall day, we all thought a picnic would be a good idea."

"Hope that's okay," Katie said.

I shrugged. "Sure, why not?"

"Great!" said Mr. Green. "Let's all walk to the park."

One of the nicest things about Maple Grove is the big park there. It has a pond and a running trail that I know Katie and her mom use all the time. When we got there we found a great tree that still had most of its bright yellow leaves. Mr. Green spread out a picnic blanket and Mrs. Brown placed the basket on it.

"We're going to take a little walk first," said Mrs. Brown. "Just don't leave the park without telling us, okay?"

"Okay, Mom," Katie said, secretly rolling her eyes at me.

When they walked off, Katie and I leaned back on the blanket. The yellow leaves looked stunning against the bright blue sky. I wondered what a fabric might look like with those two colors. Could be interesting.

Then I remembered. "So, I was thinking about going to design school in Manhattan after high school," I said. "Ava and I could be roommates."

Katie frowned. "I wish I could be your roommate. But no way am I going to design school."

I sat straight up, excited. "But you wouldn't have to go to design school. There are amazing culinary schools in Manhattan. You could room with me and Ava."

"Awesome!" Katie said. "I wonder if there are business schools there, for Alexis. And whatever kind of school Emma wants to go to. I'm not so sure she wants to be a model."

"The more roommates we have, the more affordable our apartment will be," I said. "Alexis will like that."

Katie gazed up at the clouds. "Do you think we'll always be together, all of us?"

"I don't know," I answered honestly. "I hope so."

"I hope so too," Katie said.

That was the last thing either of us said for a while as we sat and watched the clouds float by.

CHAPTER 13

The Call

Over the next few weeks, the beautiful leaves fell off the trees. The air got colder, and my homework got harder. Talia started sitting at Chris's table at lunch. Yes, it was kind of a gloomy fall, but one thing kept me going: hope.

I was sure I was going to win that contest. Every time the phone rang at home, I jumped. Every time I got a text, my fingers trembled when I checked it. Every time I did homework on my laptop, I checked my e-mail, like, every five minutes.

But there was no news. I thought I might go crazy, but thankfully I had the Cupcake Club to keep me distracted. On one of those gloomy fall Fridays, we had a club meeting during lunch.

"So, we have tons of holiday jobs coming up,"

Alexis was saying. "And tomorrow we have that anniversary party for the Friedmans. Mia, did you get the right colors?"

The traditional theme for a twentieth-wedding anniversary is china (the stuff they make plates out of, not the country), and the Friedmans were setting the table with their original wedding china. The pattern had pretty violet flowers and green leaves, and we were going to try to replicate it on top of the cupcakes.

"I have to mix a couple of colors together, but I think I'll get it," I said.

"And Mom helped me make the samples last night," Katie said, taking a small plastic food container from her backpack. "The bottle of violet syrup cost about eight bucks, but we can bill them for that, can't we?"

"We charge a higher price for specialty cupcakes," Alexis reminded her. "That covers stuff like this. Can I drop one off at the Friedmans'? Mrs. Friedman wanted a taste test."

"Sure," Katie said, handing over the box. "But you guys should try them too. I think they came out nice, but they're kind of . . . flowery."

Alexis carefully took a cupcake out of the box and broke off a piece for herself, me, and Emma.

111

The cupcake did smell kind of flowery, but nice.

I took a bite. It was like no cupcake I had ever tasted before—but I liked it.

"It's really different," I said, "but yummy."

Alexis made a face. "I think it's weird," she said. "But they did want violets."

"Well, I like it," Emma said. "I'll bet you that Mrs. Friedman will too."

"Well, she'd better, because we don't have a Plan B," Alexis said with a sigh. "I really hate these last-minute orders."

"She's going to love them," Katie said. "I'm not worried."

"Okay, then," Alexis said. "Seven o'clock at Katie's house tonight, okay?"

"I can come tonight, but tomorrow I've got a catalog shoot, so I can't help with the delivery," Emma said.

Katie raised her eyebrows. "A high-heeled shoe catalog?" she teased.

Emma laughed. "No, thank goodness. It's actually winter boots! I'm excited."

"I'll practice mixing the colors at home before the meeting, to get them right," I offered. "I have the pictures of the china on my phone."

Knowing I had to get the flowers just right kind

of excited me, especially because I knew the cupcakes would be gorgeous once they were finished.

That might be why I didn't jump up from the dinner table that night when the phone rang. I was busy thinking about cupcakes. Eddie got up to answer the phone, and then the next thing I knew, he was standing next to me, holding out the handset.

"Mia, it's for you," he said with a twinkle in his eye.

My hand shaking, I took the phone from him. "Hello?"

"Hi, Mia," said a young female voice on the other end. "This is Allondra from *Teen Runway* magazine. I'm calling with some good news for you regarding the dress you entered in our fantasy dress contest."

I felt like I had an apple in my throat. "News? Yeah? R-really?" I stammered. Good news could only mean one thing—I had won!

"Mia, I'm happy to tell you that you came in third place," Allondra said.

It took a few seconds for what she said to register.

"Third place?" I croaked. My voice didn't even sound like mine. "Wow, that's, um, great."

But I was lying. It didn't feel great at all. Third place.

I had lost.

"We'll be sending you a packet in the mail," Allondra went on. "We're having a fashion show in Manhattan with the top ten designs, and there will be some exciting members of the fashion industry there. We'll give you free passes for your family and friends. You'll get all the details soon, but I wanted to congratulate you personally."

"Thank you," I said. My voice was barely a whisper now.

"Okay, talk to you soon, Mia. I loved your dress."

"Thank you. Bye." I hung up the phone. Mom, Eddie, and even Dan were staring at me.

"Third place, Mia!" Mom said in an extra-cheerful voice. "That's wonderful! You are one of the top three winners! There must have been so many people who entered."

"Yeah, that's really good," said Dan.

"We need to celebrate!" Eddie cried. "How about we all go out for ice cream?"

"I have a Cupcake meeting," I said. "But thanks, anyway."

I kind of picked at my dinner after that. I saw Mom and Eddie exchanging worried glances. Maybe they thought I was going to lose it or something. But mostly I felt kind of sad and flat.

After dinner I helped clear the table and then

got together the supplies for our Cupcake session at Katie's. Mom offered to give me a ride, and I climbed into the passenger seat next to her.

Mom looked like she was going to turn on the engine, but then she stopped.

"Mia, I hope you know how excited I am for you," she said. "I never wanted to force you to enter into a career in fashion, but ever since you were a little girl, I secretly hoped you would."

I was surprised. "You did?"

Mom nodded. "Of course, I had a clue that year when you were seven and your dad and I asked if you wanted to go to Disney World, and you told us you wanted to go clothes shopping instead," she said with a laugh. "But I'm thrilled it's something you've stuck with, and you love, and that you're talented at."

"Are you sure you're not just saying that because you're my mom?" I asked.

"That is my *professional* opinion," Mom replied. "And I think I'm a pretty good judge of talent. And those judges are too. Getting third place in the contest is amazing, Mia! You were competing against girls a few years older than you, and with more experience."

"I hadn't thought of that," I admitted.

"And even though you didn't come in first place, those fashion experts will still get to see your dress," Mom said. "And isn't that really what you wanted? To get some advice and attention for your talent? Well, you're going to get it. I am so excited for that fashion show."

Mom was starting to turn my whole head around. "Yeah, I am too," I realized.

She turned on the engine. "Your friends are going to be so happy for you. And think—you all get to go to the fashion show together."

"You're right." Suddenly, I could envision Emma walking down a runway—a real runway—in my dress! I couldn't wait.

We pulled up in front of Katie's house, and I leaned over and hugged Mom.

"Thanks," I said.

She smiled. "I'm so proud of you, Mia."

I practically ran into Katie's house.

"I got third place!" I yelled as soon as she opened the door.

Katie started screaming and jumping up and down and hugging me. Her mom came running up.

"Is everything okay?"

"Mia got third place in the design contest!" Katie squealed.

"Mia, that's wonderful!" said Mrs. Brown, giving me a hug too.

"Third place?"

Alexis and Emma had arrived and were climbing up the steps behind me.

"Third place," I repeated, and it sounded better every time I said it. "And there's going to be a fashion show, and everybody can come. Emma, I'm not sure, but I think you can model in it, but I have to ask."

"A runway show? Cool!" Emma's blue eyes were shining.

"That is great news, Mia," Alexis said.

"Well, come in, girls, come in," said Mrs. Brown. "It's chilly out here."

We headed inside Katie's house, and my friends had tons of questions for me as we set up to start our baking. The heat from the oven made the kitchen nice and toasty, and Katie started doing impressions of all our teachers, and we were laughing hard, and soon the delicious smell of cupcakes filled the air.

That's when I had a completely dorky moment.

"You know what?" I said. "At first I was kind of bummed about getting third place in the contest, but I'm already a winner, because you guys are my friends."

117

I knew the words were supercorny as soon as they came out of my mouth, but my friends didn't mind. Katie hugged me with floury hands.

"Awww, you're so sweet," she said. "That means we're all winners too, then."

Luckily, Alexis ended the sappy moment.

"Mia, if your fashion career doesn't work out, you could get a job writing greeting cards," she teased.

I playfully hit her with a dish towel. "Very funny! I don't care how it sounds. I mean it. I love you guys!"

"Group hug!" Katie yelled, and soon we were all covered with flour and sugar from one another's hands, and it was a total mess.

And I didn't mind one bit.

CHAPTER 14

"An Impeccable Eye"

Welcome, everyone, to the *Teen Runway* Design Your Fantasy Dress fashion show!"

Everyone clapped, and I nervously looked around the fancy hotel conference room, sizing up the crowd. Mom, Eddie, Dan, Katie, Alexis, Ava, and my dad and I had one row to ourselves. The other rows were filled with other contest finalists and their families. Some men in nice suits and women in chic dresses were sitting in the front rows on each side of the runway. I suspected they were the fashion experts and maybe people who worked for the magazine, but I didn't recognize any of them. Mom had waved at a couple people before we sat down.

The woman talking onstage had sleek red hair pulled back into a bun. She wore a short black dress with cap sleeves and turquoise high-heeled shoes.

"I'm Laura Arnes, the editor in chief of *Teen Runway*," she said. "When we announced this contest, we had no idea how many entries we would get from so many talented young designers. We received more than four thousand submissions."

Katie nudged me. "That means you beat out three thousand, nine hundred and ninety-seven other people!" she whispered.

I sat up proudly in my chair. Third place seemed more impressive than before.

"Our judges had a tough job trying to choose the best of the best," Laura said. "And you'll see our top ten here today. But before we show them off, let's meet some of the special guests who helped our staff judge this contest. First, fashion designer Jeremy Collins."

A twentysomething man with black eyeglasses and thick brown hair swept over his forehead gave a little wave. I almost let out a scream, but I stopped myself. Jeremy came on the scene last year, and I have been following his career ever since. His clothes are totally fun and cute, and they are always on the covers of all the magazines.

"Next is Blayne Lockery, the star of the hit television series *Young Vampires*."

A bunch of people in the crowd clapped really hard, because Blayne is pretty famous. I hadn't recognized her because her hair was in this cute, short bob, and on the show it's really long.

Ava, who was on the other side of me, noticed it too. "She must wear a wig on the show," she whispered.

"And last but not least, legendary designer Simone Veger!"

Simone got the loudest applause of all. She really is a legend. You can only find her clothes in the fanciest department stores in the city.

"And now, without further adieu, I present to you the top ten looks in our fantasy dress competition!" Laura announced, and then she climbed down from the runway.

They had told me that they were going to reveal the dresses from tenth place to first place. Loud music started blaring from the speakers, and the first model walked out.

The model was wearing a shiny silver jumpsuit with a thick band around the middle, and wide legs.

"Designer Dena Wilmore made this jumpsuit out of an unconventional material—aluminum foil," Laura narrated. "It's sure to lend shine to any night out on the town."

For the first time in my life I knew what people meant when they said, "my jaw dropped open." My mouth was open wide in shock—Katie had been right! Aluminum foil? The judges liked things that were edgy and different.

The next dress was a superpretty, flowing peasant dress with a design stitched across the bodice.

"Jordan Lynn tells us she spent thirty-six hours hand-embroidering this dress," reported Laura.

Thirty-six hours. Wow. I was really impressed.

The next few dresses were all on the ultracreative side. One had a plastic bubble skirt over white leggings. Another dress was sewn from Japanese origami paper! And I thought my satin lining was difficult.

By the time they got to my dress, I was starting to wonder how I had achieved third place. I held my breath as the model wearing the fourth-place dress finished her walk.

"Next, Mia Vélaz-Cruz gives us a sophisticated evening dress with a playful satin lining and matching cape," Laura said, and Emma stepped out onto the runway. Mom had done her hair and makeup again, and even though she was wearing the silver high heels, she managed to gracefully stroll down the runway. When she got to the end of her walk, she unbuttoned the cape and playfully tossed it over one shoulder, so people could see the reversible pink side.

"Woo-hoo!" Katie cheered next to me.

I carefully observed the judges as they watched Emma walk. I mean, I know that they already liked the dress, but this was their first time seeing it in person, and I wanted to see their reactions. I couldn't read Jeremy and Blayne, but Simone was nodding her head and smiling.

Everyone was clapping for the dress, and I felt myself blushing with pride. This was the coolest moment ever!

Then the second dress came out. "Our second-place winner is Zoey Webber, with a beautiful take on mixing materials."

It was a two-piece look, with this amazingly tailored jacket that flared out a little at the waist, paired with a long, straight skirt that looked kind of like a patchwork except all the pieces were the same color. It looked really edgy and cool, and I knew there was no way I could have made that jacket. Not without a lot more lessons from Millicent.

I heard a squeal and then turned to my left. I saw some girls hugging a pretty girl with long brown hair and side-swept bangs. I guessed that was probably Zoey Webber. She caught my eye, and we both smiled shyly at each other. Zoey pointed at Emma wearing my dress and silently mouthed, *You?* I nodded and then pointed to the second-place winner and mouthed back, *You?* She nodded, and we both giggled. Mom was right—being in the top three was awesome!

"And now our first-place dress, designed by Lauren Noll."

A tall, thin model stepped onto the runway, wearing a dress that looked like something out of a dream. It was this really pretty soft tangerine color with a tight, sleeveless bodice and a skirt that was just layers and layers of soft, fluffy tulle—or was it organza? The layers cascaded down the model's body and trailed behind her on the floor. It looked like she was wearing a tangerine cloud.

"That is fabulous!" I whispered to Ava.

Before the fashion show I sort of believed that third place was a good thing and that there were probably better entries than mine, but now I really believed it. The dress was magnificent.

The crowd applauded wildly, and then all ten models came out for one final walk. This time, Katie stood up when Emma came out, and a bunch of other people in the crowd started standing up too.

"Let's hear it for these talented young designers!"

Laura called out, and the applause got even louder.

"Just soak it all in, Mia," Ava whispered into my ear. "It doesn't get any better than this."

But guess what? It did get better. When the show was over, everybody was invited to hang out and have refreshments set up on one side of the room. Katie and Ava made a beeline for the food, Emma sat down and changed from her heels to silver flats, and Alexis started handing out business cards to everybody.

"We have experience catering for fashion shows," she was saying, which is true. (We had made cupcakes for a fashion show at the Women's Club once.)

As for me, I was busy getting squeezed by Mom, Eddie, and Dad. I am lucky that things aren't too weird with Mom and Dad since the divorce. Dad doesn't mind hanging around when Eddie's there. It's kind of nice for me to have everybody who loves me all in one place.

"I'm so proud of you, *mija*," Dad told me. "Your dress is beautiful."

"Thanks," I said. "And thanks for sending me to the program at Parsons. It really helped."

"Anything for my daughter," Dad said, hugging me again.

As I broke away from Dad, Laura Arnes walked up to me and extended her hand.

"It's so nice to meet you, Mia," she said. "Your dress was absolutely lovely. We had to acknowledge it because your sewing and instincts were impeccable, and the design was truly classic. Simone especially loved it."

"She did?" I asked, glancing over at the famous designer. She was talking to Jeremy and laughing at something he was saying.

Laura nodded. "Yes. But we were looking for a fantasy dress, and some of the girls were able to dream up some really unique and amazing designs."

"I know," I said. "Those last two dresses were spectacular."

Laura smiled. "I hope you enjoyed the show and will enter again," she said. "We here at *Teen Runway* look forward to seeing what you will create in years to come."

"I will. Thank you!" I said, and as I shook her hand once again, I suddenly realized how sweaty my palms were. But Laura was too classy to say anything; she just smiled and walked away.

Katie and Ava ran up to me.

"Wow, that is so cool!" Ava said. "The editor of *Teen Runway* just shook your hand!"

"Yeah, I guess she did," I said as the awesomeness of the whole situation just kept spreading over me.

Then I heard a voice exclaim, "Sara!"

A man wearing a blue hat with a red feather in it walked right toward my mom. I recognized him right away. It was Verne Garcia, another designer. His fall fashion show had been a huge hit.

"You know him?" I whispered.

Mom nodded. "I worked on several of his shows," she said, and then she smiled and extended her hand. "Verne, so good to see you!"

"Pleasure," Verne said, giving her a kiss on the cheek.

Then he looked at me.

"You didn't tell me you had a budding designer in your house," he said. He leaned over to me. "Don't worry. . . . Some of these crazy outfits definitely took skill, but they aren't wearable at all. I mean, who's going to wear an outfit that's made out of aluminum foil? You, my dear, have an impeccable eye for what a woman would actually buy. A truly marketable skill, and a rare one, too. I'm going to keep my eye on you!"

"Thanks!" I said, and I felt a perma-grin appear on my face as he waved and walked away. Verne Garcia was going to keep an eye on *me*. Me!

"You know, that's very true, Mia," Mom said. "It's a good lesson, too. Some fashion is for appreciation, and some fashion is for wearing."

I thought about it. "That makes sense," I said. "I guess the fashion appreciation stuff gets more attention."

"Yes, and to be fair, the designs that won had an incredible amount of talent behind them," Mom pointed out. "But you are a little more practical. That's not a bad thing."

"Did somebody say practical?" Alexis asked, walking up to us. "That makes sense to me."

"Me too," said Katie, looking down at her jeans. "My whole wardrobe is practical. And stained."

We all laughed.

"I can't think of anything that could make this day any better," I said with a happy sigh.

"I can," said Katie.

I raised an eyebrow. "Oh? What's that?"

Katie grinned. "Cupcakes!"

"Three cheers for Mia!" Katie cried, holding out her cupcake.

After the fashion show, we had said good-bye to Dad and Ava, and Mom, Eddie, Dan, and I headed back home with the rest of the Cupcake

Club. Then we all went to Katie's house. To surprise me, she had decorated her living room with gray and pink streamers and a big sign that read, CONGRATULATIONS, MIA!

Not only that, but Katie, Emma, and Alexis had baked me a special batch of cupcakes, with icing the same gray as my dress, and a perfect pink flower on top of each one.

Mrs. Brown and Mr. Green joined us, and everyone held up a cupcake for a toast.

"Mia! Mia! Mia!" everyone cheered.

"Thanks!" I said. "Here's to coming in third."

"You know, top three is pretty darn good," said Katie. "I mean, you guys are my top three friends."

I giggled. "And you three are my top three friends."

"Mine too!" said Alexis.

"Ditto!" added Emma, and we all collapsed into giggles.

Katie's mom motioned to the adults. "Let's head into the kitchen for coffee. You can come too, Dan."

"Thanks," my stepbrother replied. "It's getting way too girlie in here."

I sat down on Katie's comfy couch and unwrapped my cupcake. The pleats on the wrapper reminded me of a pleated skirt.

"Hey!" I cried. "What about a dress made entirely out of cupcake wrappers?"

"Oh my gosh! That's genius!" Katie cried.

Alexis nodded. "Cupcake fashion. Could be a nice business tie-in."

"Well," said Emma. "Considering what happened this time, maybe you should stay clear of mixing cupcakes with fabric."

"Good point," said Katie. "Unless wearing frosting is part of the design."

I laughed. It felt good to joke about the disaster now. And besides, that catastrophe made me rethink the design and be open to other suggestions. All things Mom said were really important for being a fashion designer.

I was glad that the contest was over and that I could just hang out with my friends again. It had been a pretty stressful few weeks. Third place wasn't what I originally planned for, but it turned out to be a pretty big deal. As I bit into the delicious cupcake, I realized that sometimes things don't exactly go as planned, and they don't end perfectly, but sometimes they end up sweeter in the end.

Want another sweet cupcake?
Here's a sneak peek
of the next book in the

Cupcake  Diaries

series:

Emma's
not-so-sweet
dilemma

emma

Baking Hazard

My alarm went off and I hit snooze, even though I was already more than half awake. The Cupcake Club was coming over pretty early this morning to work out the kinks in a new recipe we were creating for a holiday boutique we were participating in, and I was looking forward to it. I snuggled deep under my covers and wiggled my toes in their fluffy pink socks. But I dreaded getting out of bed, even though it was a Saturday. It had been so freezing cold for the past week that I'd been walking around like a mummy in layers and layers of clothes (sleeping in socks and long flannel pj's), and to leave my cocoon of blankets this morning would be unbearable.

But then I noticed something. I could smell!

I'd been suffering from a terrible cold for the past week, and my nose had been totally stuffed up. I couldn't even taste the cupcakes we made at our last Cupcake meeting, never mind smell them cooking. (Katie was raving about the aroma, and I felt totally left out!) But now my cold seemed like it was nearly gone, and I could smell the pancakes my mom was making downstairs. Their scent floated under the crack in my door, across the room, and tickled my nose, like in a cartoon. Cold or no, I had to have them!

I braced myself, flopped back the covers, and launched out of bed. My dad insists on keeping the heat lower than most normal people would. ("Just put on a sweater!" he grumps when I'm sitting at my desk doing homework, my nose red and running from the cold.) But today I am already noticing it must be warmer outside, because when I opened my bedroom door, I didn't have the sensation that I was entering a walk-in freezer. This day just kept getting better and better!

Downstairs, my mom was listening to an author being interviewed on public radio while she bustled around the kitchen making breakfast. Besides pancakes there were hard-boiled eggs with sea salt, fruit salad, and fresh-squeezed orange juice.

"Mama!" I squealed, using my baby name for her. "What's the occasion?"

"Good morning, sweetheart!" my mom said cheerily. She put down the pan she was drying with a dish towel. "The occasion is that it will break forty degrees today! It's summer!" she joked.

"Wow, maybe I'll go to the beach," I said, and we both laughed. "What's up for today? The girls are coming over in half an hour to bake. We're going to need the kitchen, please."

"Okay. That's fine. Let's see. Matt should be home from practice with Dad any minute. Jake has a playdate at eleven. Sam is actually around today; he's working the night shift at the theater, because he's got to study for exams. So a busy morning but probably a quiet afternoon around here." She put a plate down in front of me. It had a steaming stack of chocolate chip pancakes on it that looked like ginormous chocolate chip cookies.

"Mmmm!" My mouth was watering. I sliced off a huge pat of butter and slathered it in between the pancakes, where it quickly melted and pooled. When I took my first bite, the saltiness of the butter and the sweetness of the pancake combined with the sharp chocolate, forming an ideal swirl in my mouth.

"Oh, Mom!" I moaned. "These are soooo good! Thank you for making them!"

My mom smiled. "Glad you like them."

"We should really do a chocolate chip pancake cupcake. I need to get Katie on it. She's so good at figuring out what you need to do to make something taste like something else. Sometimes you almost have to trick your mouth. It's cool how she knows what to do." I took a big swig of orange juice and returned to the pancake stack.

"What was that new holiday cupcake you were working on last week? That one sounded delicious," my mom said enthusiastically.

"Well, there were two, actually. One was a cherry cupcake with pistachio frosting, so it's red and green for Christmas—get it? The other was blue and white for Hanukkah. The blue frosting was peppermint and the white cake was vanilla. It's a great combo. Kind of like peppermint stick ice cream. I think we've got the Hanukkah one down, but we're going to be tinkering with the red and green one today. My nose was so stuffed up last week, I couldn't taste anything, so at this meeting I think I'll be more helpful." I inhaled deeply through my nose, and my mom smiled again.

"Back to normal?"

"Almost. Much better, anyway. It was such a drag being sick."

Just then my dad and Matt walked in.

"Awesome!" cried Matt, running to the stovetop where my mom had a tall stack of pancakes keeping warm. He reached his hands out to grab one off the top, but my mom was there in a flash.

"Not so fast, mister! Wash those hands first!"

The boys' hands are always supergross when they get home from practice, no matter what sport it is. And they play every sport. Lucky me.

Matt rolled his eyes and reluctantly went to the sink. "Can I have six, please, Mom?" he asked.

"Must've been a big practice!" My mom laughed.

"Wait, can you save a couple for the Cupcake Clubbers, please?" I asked.

"I have lots more batter, so don't worry," said my mom. "I'll make a few more and keep them warm in the oven, then I'll clear out, so you can have the kitchen all to yourselves."

"The Cupcake Club is meeting here today? Oh, great." Matt groaned, tucking into his pancake stack (with a fork this time). But he didn't look too upset about it. My friends are really cute and my BFF, Alexis Becker, has a major crush on Matt. They've even had some mild date-y interaction, which for me is cool and annoying all at the same time.

"You know you love it when we're here," I teased.

"Not," said Matt.

"Well, you certainly love the free cupcake samples!"

"Yeah, but I take my life in my hands every time I try one!"

"Well, if you think we're such bad bakers, maybe you don't need to sample anything or hang around my cute friends this morning. Huh? How do you like that?"

"No need to get all huffy," said Matt.

I knew I'd backed him into a corner, so I decided for one final push. "Go ahead and apologize and maybe I'll reconsider."

Matt scoffed, but then after a pause he said, "I'm sorry you're such bad bakers."

"Matthew!" warned my mom, but she was laughing.

"Seriously? And you think I'm going to . . ."

"Stop, Em. I'm just kidding. I'm sorry. You are

baking goddesses. The best in the universe, okay? Now just make sure to throw me a few free samples today. That's all. A growing boy's gotta eat."

"Yeah. A knuckle sandwich maybe," I muttered.

"Mom! Did you hear her? And you and Dad always think she's the innocent one around here!" protested Matt. He shook his head vehemently. "Always the victim. And we're always the bad guys."

"Well, you did start it!" I said.

"Hellooooo?" called someone from the mudroom, and Alexis appeared. A huge grin spread across her face when she spotted Matt.

I glanced at Matt to see his reaction and annoyingly enough, his face had lit up too. He was psyched to see Alexis.

"Hey, Lexi," I said, bounding off my stool at the counter. "Come see my . . . new winter skirt. In my room. It's so cute. I made it in my home ec class. I might wear it to the holiday boutique."

Her smile faded a bit. "Okay . . . cool."

I didn't watch to see if she and Matt exchanged any looks of longing, because I would have puked.

We headed upstairs, and soon after, Katie Brown and Mia Vélaz-Cruz came up to meet us. I showed them my new skirt, and Mia, ever the fashionista (even with a homemade skirt to work with!) helped me put together three different looks with it. Since everyone had arrived, we popped down to the kitchen to get to work, with my mom's chocolate chip pancakes to energize us.

We chatted about how warm it was going to be outside for a change (sixty degrees, which is totally crazy for this time of year) while I gathered our supplies and Alexis busied herself with our ledger, where we keep track of our profits and expenses and plans. Katie laid out her idea book, which was battered and stained and laden with awesome recipes, and Mia pulled up photos of some inspirational cupcakes on her tablet.

"Okay, here's the key, girls!" Katie withdrew a little bag from her tote and opened it. Inside were a few ingredients. We clustered around while she showed us.

"Dried cherries, pistachios, cherry jam, and—drumroll, please!—pistachio pudding!"

"Okay!" I said enthusiastically. "So what do we do?"

Katie explained how the dried cherries and pistachios needed to be rough chopped, which means chopped really coarsely, and how we would be incorporating the pistachio pudding mix into our yellow cake cupcake recipe, along with some of the cherries. Then we'd swirl the cherry jam though a cream cheese frosting base and sprinkle the frosted cakes with the crushed pistachios. We all took a task and got to work, chatting as we chopped and mixed and measured.

Jake and Sam both arrived and passed through, looking for swabs of frosting on a spoon or a lick of batter, but we shooed them away, with Mia (too generous always!) promising to bring them samples when the cakes were ready.

"Hmph!" I said. "You spoil them."

"It's fun." Mia laughed, her dark eyes twinkling merrily. "They're so appreciative of our baking!"

The cupcakes were soon in the oven, and I couldn't stop taking big gulping whiffs of delicious air through my newly cleared nose. It was like I'd been at sea for months and could finally smell land again. The girls teased me, but I didn't mind. The cherry and pistachio cupcakes smelled wonderful. While we waited for them to come out, and then to cool, we made the frosting and brainstormed about our holiday shopping.

"Everything seems so expensive to me this year,"

said Katie, her brow furrowing anxiously. She was whipping up cream cheese frosting in the mixer as I chopped pistachios.

"I know," I agreed. "I was at the mall the other day because the boys had to go to the sporting goods store, and even the sneakers there . . . it seems like the prices have just jumped all of a sudden."

"Yeah, we need to make some money. Do you have any modeling jobs lined up, Em?" asked Alexis. (I model for a few local businesses, but mostly for a bridal store at the mall owned by a really nice lady named Mona.)

"Not at the moment," I said. "I'm hoping Mona will have something soon. I know there's a new line she's hoping to get, so maybe. . . . The extra money sure would help."

"I'm hoping we'll find some cute things at the holiday boutique," said Mia.

The boutique is an annual tradition. It's held in the basement of our local Y, and lots of vendors come from all around with beautiful, mostly handmade and one of a kind, items that make great holiday gifts. Candles, potpourri, customized stationery, needlepoint canvases and yarn, hand-knit scarves and gloves, fabric coin purses, special chocolates, fudge, and more. We would be selling cupcakes this year at a table in the refreshments area on the opening Saturday of the fair. It was a pretty big honor to be asked to participate, and that's why we wanted our holiday-themed cupcakes to be special.

While we chatted about who was on our lists to buy holiday gifts for (my list had my brothers, my parents, Mona at the bridal salon, and the Cupcakers, of course!), the cupcakes came out of the oven, and Mia placed them carefully onto the wire racks to cool. Meanwhile, Katie carefully tipped three or four drops of green food coloring into the cream cheese frosting, then mixed it until it came out a delicate green.

I set the bowl of chopped pistachios next to the icing, and we were ready to frost. Just then the boys came swarming back though the kitchen.

"Yum! Mia! Can I have a cupcake now? Pretty pleeeeease?" begged Jake.

Mia crouched down, looking at him with sorrow, and said, "They're not ready yet, Jake! We're going to frost them, and then you can have a couple, okay?"

reach maximum swelling through tomorrow, and then that will start to calm down, but don't be surprised when the black eyes appear tomorrow or the next day. Those can take a while to fade, too."

"Oh, great," I said sarcastically.

He looked at me sympathetically. "I know. It really is a drag, but it could have been a lot worse. Your nose didn't even break. You've been drinking your milk!"

He looked at his watch, and we all stood up.

Then he continued, "I'm very glad you don't have a concussion, Emma. I've had kids out of school for weeks because they'd get a migraine every time they looked at a white sheet of paper. And that meant while they were home, no TV, no computer, and no phone. Nothing to overstimulate or irritate the brain. Trust me, it's just awful. I hate to see it."

"I know. I'm glad about I avoided that too."

"Just ice the nose a lot, drink tons of water, and take aspirin, and you'll be just fine."

We thanked him and headed out to the car.

In the car, my mom said, "Well, that's a relief."

"I guess," I said, lowering the visor and flipping open the mirror. I took a deep breath through my mouth and braced myself.

And then I took one look at my bashed-up face and burst into tears. It was awful. I had a huge bump across the bridge of my nose, and the skin was broken and bloody, and a huge dark blue bruise was smeared across my nose, and even starting under my eyes. But what was worse was the swelling. I looked like an alien. The center of my face, including my nose and the area between my eyebrows, was so swollen that the space between the inside corners of my eyes had doubled.

"OMG." I began to sob, which of course made my nose hurt more and my face look even uglier. "I'm not going to be able to leave the house for weeks!" I wailed.

My mom put her arm around me and hugged me tightly. "I think you're going to have to wear a hat and maybe some sunglasses for a few days," she whispered into my hair.

"More like for the rest of my life!" I whimpered.

"One!" I said sternly.

"But we're going outside now, to play football . . . ," pressed Jake.

"I'll bring them out to you. Now, shoo! Be gone!" I whisked them out the back door before my co-clubbers had a chance to offer any more free food to them. I shut the back door hard and could hear the boys laughing outside. "Scoundrels!" I scoffed.

"You know you're lucky to have them, Em," said Mia, laughing.

"Yes, I would love to live with Matt," joked Alexis.

I rolled my eyes.

Katie said, "It's nice to have such good eaters around, anyway. When I bake at home, my mom might try a tiny bite, and even if she loves it, she doesn't have more. These guys go crazy for what we make."

"I guess," I said.

"Come on, they're not that bad," said Mia. "Remember the time Matt made those flyers for us on his computer?"

"Yeah," agreed Alexis. "And how he always picks hanging with us over the so-called popular girls?"

"And the time Sam drove us to the mall to get your bridesmaid dress . . ."

"Which Matt paid for!"

I put up my hands, giggling. "All right, all right. I surrender. They're not that bad. They're pretty good, actually."

We were all laughing.

"Now fork over some of them cupcakes, and I'll bring them out," I joked to Katie.

Smiling, she quickly frosted six, and then Mia sprinkled them with the nuts. I put them on a plate and headed out the back door, calling, "Cupcakes! Come and get 'em!" to the boys.

But just as I rounded the corner, tragedy struck.

Tragedy in the form of a very large, very hard, very out-of-control football.

It hit me square in the nose, and I remember an instant shock and pain, and that's all.

Sooner or Later

$\mathscr{I}$ came to on the sofa in the TV room, with everyone gathered anxiously around me. I wasn't sure where I was at first. People around me were speaking in hushed voices.

"Her eyes are open!"

"She's awake!"

"Okay, okay, shh. Shh, everyone." My mom sat forward and smoothed back my hair, looking at me carefully as she lifted a cold compress from my face.

"Oh no!" cried Jake.

I sat up quickly, but my mom pushed me back gently. "Stay put. Just rest."

"What happened? Ow!" I moaned. My face was throbbing, and it felt hot and kind of tight. I reached up a hand to gingerly touch my nose. "OMG. This kills."

"Emmy! I'm so sorry! I threw it! It's all my fault!" Jake wailed, in floods of tears now.

"Stop crying!" Matt said sharply. "This isn't about you!" He looked scared himself.

Jake tried to calm down, but tears kept streaming down his cheeks and he hiccupped. He had obviously been crying hard for some time.

"How did I get here?" I asked, looking around. Everyone's face was superworried, especially the Cupcakers.

"You were coming out with the cupcakes, and we were having a contest to see who could throw the ball the hardest and Jake was just taking his turn. It hit you square on the bridge of your nose," said Sam. "I'm so sorry."

"Oh no!" I groaned. "Is it broken?"

"I don't think so," said my mom. With me having three brothers, she's seen a lot of injuries. "I'm more worried about you losing consciousness. We've got to go see the doctor and make sure it's not a concussion. I already have a call in to him."

"Wait, I blacked out?" I said. "I've never done that before."

"We carried you in," said Matt. "It was scary."

"Thanks. Sorry." I shrugged.

My mom dabbed at my nose with a wet paper towel. I could see that it already had quite a bit of blood on it. My stomach churned. I hate the sight of blood.

"Do you have a headache, sweetheart?" she asked.

"No, I have a nose ache," I said.

"Do you feel queasy?"

"Not really."

"Good," said my mom, patting my arm.

"Can I look in a mirror?" I asked.

"No," said everyone all at once. Then they laughed nervously, but I didn't.

"That bad, huh?" I asked.

The Cupcakers smiled supportively, but I caught Jake nodding before Matt spied him and quickly tapped him on the back of his head. Then Jake started shaking his head.

"Oooh." I groaned. "Good thing I don't have any modeling jobs lined up. Hey, how were the cupcakes?" I asked.

"We didn't have the stomach to try them . . . ," explained Sam.

"I ate one! I thought it was delicious!" said Jake.

Mia smiled at him and gave him a sideways hug, "You're our best little customer, aren't you?"

He nodded, in heaven. "Can I have another?"

Mia laughed. "And an opportunist, too! Sure, come on, let's go get you another."

"Hey, wait up!" called Sam. "Feel better, Em," he said with a wink, and he headed into the kitchen.

Matt trailed behind them, and my mom went to call the doctor again. I was left with Alexis and Katie. "How bad is it?" I whispered, now kind of dreading seeing it.

"Oh, you know . . . ," said Katie vaguely.

Alexis set her lips in a grim line. "You're going to look awful for a few days. But then it will be fine. No permanent damage."

"Alexis!" said Katie, shocked at her bluntness.

"What?" said Alexis, huffy now. "It's true. Why should I lie to her?"

"Hey, no. It's fine. I wanted the truth," I said. "It's better to know. I'll see it, anyway, sooner or later, right?" I reached up to try to feel around, and I could definitely feel the swelling all across my face. "Ugh."

"Yeah, better if later," agreed Alexis. "Rather

than sooner, I mean." She glanced guiltily at Katie, who just shook her head.

My mom came bustling back in. "Okay, the doctor can take a look at you if we head over now. Are you okay to try to sit up?"

I swung my legs over the side of the sofa and sat up tall, but I suddenly got a head rush, and things were a little spinny for a minute. I glanced at my mom, and her face was really worried, so I tried to pull it together for her sake, anyway. I took a deep breath.

"Okay," I said.

Soon I was up on my feet and walking a little wobbly out to the car, the Cupcakers trailing behind.

"We'll just clean up here, then head out, so you can come home and rest," said Alexis from the back door.

"And we'll walk Jake to his playdate," added Mia. My mom thanked her.

"No, feel free to stay. I won't be long." We were supposed to head to Scoops ice-cream shop for grilled cheese and milkshakes later. "We can go after."

Alexis grimaced. "I don't know if you're going

to want to go out when you get back," she said, shrugging helplessly.

I sat down in the backseat of the minivan. "Oh boy," I said.

Alexis gave a sigh. "Just don't look in the mirror."

She was right.

On the way to the doctor's I couldn't face my reflection. I was worried if it looked really bad, I wouldn't want to get out of the car. The doctor was supernice, and he gave me all sorts of funny tests, asking me things like what the date was a week ago on Thursday and to do some simple puzzles and stuff, and he concluded that I did not have a concussion, which was my mom's main concern.

"The site of the impact is a factor," he told my mom. "And noses absorb a lot of impact. Two inches higher . . ." And then he shrugged. "One thing's for sure, Emma. Your brain should be grateful to your nose. It really took one on the chin today!" Then he laughed at his own bad joke.

I smiled. "I guess," I said. "But how bad is this nose going to look and for how long?" I tried not to whine, but I was worried.

He shook his head. "Hard to say. You'll probably

Want more

CUPCAKE DIARIES?

Visit **CupcakeDiariesBooks.com**
for the series trailer, excerpts, activities,
and everything you need for throwing
your own cupcake party!

Alexis Gets Frosted 12

Katie's New Recipe 13

Mia a Matter of Taste 14

Emma Sugar and Spice and Everything Nice 15

Alexis and the Missing Ingredient 16

Katie Sprinkles & Surprises 17

Mia Fashion Plates and Cupcakes 18

Emma: Lights! Camera! Cupcakes! 19

Alexis the Icing on the Cupcake 20

Katie Starting from Scratch 21

Mia's Recipe for Disaster 22

Emma's Not-So-Sweet Dilemma 23

Coco Simon always dreamed of opening a cupcake bakery but was afraid she would eat all of the profits. When she's not daydreaming about cupcakes, Coco edits children's books and has written close to one hundred books for children, tweens, and young adults, which is a lot less than the number of cupcakes she's eaten. Cupcake Diaries is the first time Coco has mixed her love of cupcakes with writing.